The Faces

Behind

The Father

By

J.Outis

Prologue

A Letter to My Son

Dear Son,

As I write this, my heart is heavy yet hopeful. There is so much I want to tell you, so much I want to prepare you for. You see, I've lived my life carrying something that I once believed was a curse—a burden that left me confused, isolated, and unsure of who I was. I was diagnosed with multiple personality disorder, a condition that shattered my sense of self and left me battling with what felt like different versions of me, all competing for control.

I don't know for certain if this was caused by the trauma I endured during my childhood. My early years were anything but easy—marked by hardship, pain, and an overwhelming sense of instability. I didn't have the guidance or comfort that every child deserves, and those experiences left deep scars. But I've also come to learn that this condition may be genetic, a part of me that I inherited and now see glimpses of in you.

If this same thing happens to you, I want you to know this: you are not alone. This book is my way of giving you the guidance I never had, a roadmap to navigate the complexities of a condition that can feel overwhelming but also holds incredible potential. I've lived with it, fought with it, and, over time, learned to master it. What I once thought of as a curse, I now see as a gift—a unique ability to perceive the world through multiple lenses and respond to it in extraordinary ways.

But this gift is a double-edged sword. Left unchecked, it can consume you. During your teenage years, you may begin to notice the signs—extreme shifts in behavior, thoughts, or emotions that feel like they're coming from someone else entirely. Pay attention to these moments, not with fear, but with awareness. They are clues, pieces of the puzzle that is you.

This book is my way of ensuring you are equipped to embrace this gift, temper its extremes, and channel its power in ways that benefit your life rather than hinder it. I will share the pros and cons, the strengths and pitfalls, and, most importantly, the lessons I've learned about how to utilize this ability to its fullest.

My greatest wish is to give you the tools to thrive in ways I couldn't when I was your age. To help you see that you are not broken—you are extraordinary. And to remind you, always, that you are deeply loved, just as you are.

You are my legacy, my greatest joy, and my enduring hope. Wherever life takes you, know that I am always with you—in these words, in your heart, and in the strength you carry within.

With all my love,

Your Father

Discovering the Gift

Chapter 1: The Shadow Within

The Shadow Within

They say every person carries shadows within them, pieces of themselves they can't fully understand. But what if those shadows had voices? What if they had personalities, desires, and motives of their own?

For most of my life, I didn't understand what was happening to me. I wasn't just one person. I was many. The world around me seemed like a puzzle, and my mind was a kaleidoscope of shifting patterns and colors, trying to interpret it. There were times when I'd wake up unsure of where I'd been or what I'd done. Moments of brilliance were followed by stretches of emptiness as if someone else had taken over my body and left me as a spectator.

As a child, I thought everyone experienced the world like this. Didn't everyone hear the conflicting whispers of different parts of themselves? Didn't everyone have moments of rage so consuming it blackened out the world or joy so intense it felt like flying too close to the sun? It wasn't until I got older that I realized I was different—different in ways I didn't understand, ways that scared me.

I didn't have a name for it back then. The world didn't offer me a diagnosis or a roadmap. All I had were questions and the weight of those shadows pressing down on me. It wasn't until much later that I came to understand what was happening. I had what doctors would call **Dissociative Identity Disorder**, a condition often tied to trauma, though its roots are not always so clear.

And yet, even that label never felt quite right to me.

This isn't a disorder, not in the way most people think. It's an extraordinary ability—one that comes with risks, yes, but also immense potential. The personas within me, born from different facets of my experiences and emotions, have given me perspectives and abilities that I might never have accessed otherwise. Each one has its strengths, its weaknesses, and its place in my life.

But it wasn't always this way. For a long time, I saw these personas as a curse. They fractured my sense of self, pulling me in directions I couldn't control. I felt like a passenger in my own life, watching helplessly as my actions—driven by a part of me I didn't recognize—hurt those around me and sabotaged my future. I lived in fear of myself, unsure when Wrath might lash out, when Lust might take the reins, or when Pride might blind me to my own flaws.

Then came the breaking point.

I hit rock bottom more than once. Each time, it felt like the end—like I would never piece myself back together. But in those moments of despair, I began to see the truth: I wasn't broken. I wasn't cursed. I was *different*. And difference, as I've learned, is not the same as weakness.

This book is a deeply personal journey, a reflection on how I've learned to live with and even embrace the many facets of myself. It's also a legacy for you, my son.

I write this because I've learned that this might not be just *my* story. There's a chance that what lives within me could live within you, too. Genetics are a strange and powerful thing. I don't know for certain if this will manifest in your life, but if it does, I want you to be prepared. I want you to know that you're not alone and that this is not something to fear.

When I was young, no one could guide me through this maze. I was left to stumble through it alone, to learn the hard way which paths led to ruin and which led to growth. But you, my son—you won't have to walk this road without a map.

This book is that map.

Within these pages, I'll share everything I've learned—the mistakes I made, the lessons I gleaned, and the ways I've turned what I once thought was a curse into one of my greatest gifts. I'll show you how to harness the power of your personas, how to navigate the chaos they bring, and how to live a life of balance and purpose.

I'll also teach you how to spot the signs early. Teenage years can be a turbulent time for anyone, but for someone like us, they are especially critical. The decisions you make during this time can shape the rest of your life. It's easy to let the personas consume you, to lose yourself in their extremes. But it's also possible to master them, to find harmony between them, and to use their unique strengths to build a life that is richer, fuller, and more meaningful than you ever thought possible.

This isn't just a guide—it's a promise.

I promise you that you are not broken. You are not cursed. You are extraordinary.

And together, through these words, we'll uncover the strength within the shadows.

The Origin of the Void

"The mind has its secrets, and sometimes, it chooses to hide them even from ourselves."

It began when I was 14—a year that, by all accounts, should have passed like any other, unmarked and unexceptional. My life at the time was a meticulously constructed routine, each day a series of deliberate steps toward a future that everyone but me seemed to have already mapped out.

Mornings began early, the alarm clock's shrill call breaking the stillness of the house. By 6:30, I was on the tennis court, gripping my racket like a lifeline as my father barked corrections from the sideline. Afternoons were consumed by the precision of numbers, my hours spent hunched over math problems that required as much grit as they did genius. In between, school filled the gaps—a stage where I played the role of the "gifted student," applauded for every achievement as if I had mastered not just equations but life itself.

To the outside world, I was the golden child. My teachers beamed when they spoke of me, their praise flowing freely as they recounted my academic feats. My math coach called me his "star," his pride barely hidden as I dominated competition after competition. And my father—oh, my father—looked at me with a gleam in his eye as if I were a prodigy born to carry the dreams he had long since abandoned.

But what they saw wasn't the truth. It wasn't even close.

Beneath that carefully crafted exterior, something had begun to stir. It started so faintly that I barely noticed it at first, like the low hum of an untuned instrument buried under the noise of everyday life. For months, it was easy to dismiss—a fleeting unease, a shadow that passed too quickly to be named. But as the weeks stretched into months, the hum grew louder. It didn't just whisper; it pressed against the edges of my mind, demanding to be heard.

That was when I first encountered the void.

The Shape of Emptiness

I didn't have a name for it then. It wasn't a presence, not exactly—it felt more like an absence, a vast emptiness that existed just beyond the borders of my thoughts. It wasn't something I could touch or see, but I could feel it, pulling at me like gravity. At first, I thought it was exhaustion. After all, who wouldn't feel drained juggling the expectations of school, tennis, and the relentless grind of proving their worth? But this was different.

The void wasn't tired. It was hungry.

I remember the first time I truly noticed it. I had just finished a grueling tennis match, my father's voice ringing in my ears as he dissected every flaw in my performance. My body was slick with sweat, my muscles trembling from the effort, but as I sat on the bench, staring at the scuffed lines of the court, a strange stillness came over me. It wasn't relief, and it wasn't pride—it was nothing.

Nothingness isn't something most people can understand. It's not the same as peace or calm. It's heavier, darker, and utterly consuming. As I sat there, I felt as though I were slipping away, my thoughts unraveling into that empty space where nothing mattered—not the match, not my father's words, not even the ache in my arms. It was as if I had become untethered from myself, floating in a vacuum I couldn't escape.

A Fractured Mirror

For weeks, the void became my shadow, lurking at the edges of my awareness. It was there in the quiet moments when the noise of life faded, and I was left alone with my thoughts. It didn't always feel threatening; sometimes, it was almost comforting, like sinking into a deep, dreamless sleep. But other times, it terrified me.

I began to notice strange gaps in my memory. I couldn't recall all of the conversations, assignments I didn't remember completing, and decisions I couldn't explain. My math coach once praised me for solving a problem no one else could, but when I looked at my own work, the solution felt alien, as if someone else had written it.

And then there were the emotions—intense, uncontrollable, and utterly unpredictable. One moment, I would feel a rage so consuming it left me trembling, my vision tunneling as I struggled to keep it contained. The next, I would be overcome by an almost euphoric joy so powerful it felt like I could do anything, be anyone. And then, without warning, I would crash into despair, the weight of it dragging me down into the depths of the void once more.

I began to feel like a fractured mirror, each piece reflecting a different version of myself. And yet, none of them felt like the real me.

What the Void Demanded

I wanted to ask someone for help, but how could I explain what I didn't understand? How could I put into words the feeling of being haunted by something that wasn't even there? I tried to bury it, to push it down beneath the surface and pretend I was fine. But the void wasn't something I could ignore.

It grew stronger the more I resisted, its pull becoming impossible to deny. I would lie awake at night, staring at the ceiling as it whispered to me—not in words, but in sensations I couldn't name. It wanted something from me, though I didn't know what.

And then, one day, I realized the void wasn't empty.

It was only the beginning.

The Forgotten Hours

The first signs of the void were whispers at the edge of my consciousness—so faint, so fleeting, that I mistook them for nothing more than the fog of a busy mind. It began with the kind of forgetfulness anyone might shrug off: misplacing my tennis racket after practice, forgetting the solution to a geometry problem I had solved a hundred times before. I told myself it was normal. Who wouldn't falter under the weight of academics, athletics, and endless math drills?

But as the days slipped by, those lapses grew. The gaps in my memory widened, subtle at first, like hairline cracks in a dam. I ignored them, even as they stretched further, holding fast to the belief that I was simply tired and overworked.

And then, one Thursday, I could no longer ignore it.

The Day Begins Like Any Other

That morning started with the usual rush: cereal eaten too quickly to taste, a geometry test where the formulas seemed to blur together, and then hours on the tennis court, the afternoon sun beating down like a hammer.

My father was there, of course, standing on the sidelines with the sharp, assessing gaze of someone who expected nothing less than perfection. Every missed serve, every weak backhand, drew his disapproval, his head shaking with frustration he didn't bother to hide. He didn't yell—he never yelled. His silence was worse.

By the time practice ended, sweat soaked through my shirt, my arms trembling from exertion, I was exhausted. My body screamed for rest, but my day wasn't even close to over.

I packed my tennis bag, barely feeling my fingers, and rushed to my math training session. I arrived late, breathless, with an apology tumbling out before I even stepped through the door. My coach, immune to my fatigue, handed me a stack of combinatorics problems without a second glance. He launched into the day's lesson, his voice a monotone rhythm that barely registered as I stared at the equations in front of me.

The numbers swam on the page. My pencil hovered, motionless, as I tried to summon the energy to focus.

And then—nothing.

The Lost Hours

The next thing I knew, I was standing in my bathroom at home.

The fluorescent light above the mirror flickered; its weak hum was the only sound in the room. My hand trembled slightly as I stared at the toothbrush I didn't remember picking up. My reflection stared back, pale and gaunt, my eyes rimmed with shadows that hinted at days of sleeplessness.

The clock on the wall read 9:45 pm.

My stomach dropped. What had happened to the hours between math training and this moment?

I gripped the edge of the sink, trying to steady myself as my mind scrambled to fill in the blanks. What had I done after leaving the math center? Had I come straight home? Had I spoken to anyone? Had I eaten dinner?

There was nothing.

No fleeting images. No muffled sounds. No faint traces of where I'd been or what I'd done. My memory was a void—a perfect, impenetrable black hole that had swallowed the evening whole.

Rationalizing the Unthinkable

At first, I tried to dismiss it.

You're overtired, I told myself. *You probably zoned out while brushing your teeth and scared yourself.* But even as the thought crossed my mind, I didn't believe it. This wasn't zoning out. This wasn't just forgetting where I left my shoes or what page I'd bookmarked in my physics textbook. This was something deeper, something darker.

I leaned closer to the mirror, searching my own eyes for an answer I didn't want to find. My breath fogged the glass as my mind clawed at the empty spaces, desperate to uncover even the smallest fragment of those missing hours. But there was nothing—no hints, no echoes, no trails leading me back to the time I'd lost.

I splashed cold water on my face, the shock jolting my senses, but it did nothing to calm the unease twisting in my gut. I glanced at my reflection again, half expecting the glass to reveal something else—someone else—looking back.

The Whisper of Something More

I didn't tell anyone about it. What could I have said? My father would have dismissed it as an excuse, my coach wouldn't have cared, and my friends… Well, I wasn't sure they would understand.

So, I buried it.

For days, I tried to forget, forcing myself to focus on my routines. But the memory of that blank space lingered, as vivid as any scar. I couldn't stop thinking about the hours I'd lost, and with each passing day, the gaps in my mind seemed to grow.

I'd forget small things at first: the name of a classmate I saw every day, the details of a homework assignment I'd just written down. Then came the bigger lapses—whole conversations I couldn't recall, notes in my handwriting I didn't remember writing.

And through it all, the void waited, silent but persistent.

It wasn't just an absence anymore. It was a presence, something I could feel lurking in the back of my mind, watching, waiting. I could almost hear it whispering to me, though I couldn't make out the words.

I told myself it was stress. I told myself it would pass. But deep down, I knew the truth: the void wasn't going away.

That Thursday was just the beginning.

The Notebook

The unraveling didn't happen all at once. It was slow, like the gradual loosening of a thread until the whole fabric began to come apart. The first thread slipped free a week later, on a quiet Saturday, when I found the notebook.

I wasn't looking for anything unusual that day. My tennis bag had been sitting in the corner of my room since practice the night before, slumped over like a tired soldier. I dug through it absently, searching for my spare racket. My fingers brushed against something unexpected—something small, firm, and unfamiliar.

Pulling it out, I found a notebook.

Its black cover was worn and scuffed, the kind of texture that told a story of being carried everywhere, handled often, and perhaps forgotten just as much. There was no title, no label, no indication of what it was. I turned it over in my hands, my curiosity growing.

It didn't look like anything I recognized. I thought maybe it was an old practice schedule or some forgotten math notes. But when I opened it, I found something else entirely.

The Words That Weren't Mine

The first page hit me like a blow.

"In the spaces between breath and silence,

A voice whispers truths I cannot speak.

Who am I but fragments of shadow,

A puzzle with pieces that do not fit?"

The words blurred before my eyes as my heartbeat roared in my ears. I read the lines again and again, trying to make sense of them, but they only grew stranger with each pass.

It was my handwriting, clear as day. The slant of the letters, the slight curve of the capital "F," even the way I always crossed my T's too firmly—it was all there. And yet, these words weren't mine.

I'd never written poetry before in my life.

The lines on the page felt like a stranger's voice speaking in my hand. They carried a weight I couldn't explain, a haunting sort of rhythm that left me unsettled. And they weren't alone.

A Book of Chaos

I flipped through the notebook, my hands trembling. Every page was filled with more words, more diagrams, more art—all in my handwriting, but none of it was recognizable.

The next page held detailed diagrams of chess strategies. Precise moves, counters, and openings were laid out as though someone had been preparing for a tournament. I could see the logic behind the notes and the brilliance of the strategies, but I didn't play chess. I'd never studied it, never cared for it.

Then there were the sketches. Lifelike faces stared back at me, their expressions so vivid they seemed almost alive. A man with deep-set eyes and a weathered frown. A woman whose hair tumbled over her shoulders like a river, her gaze piercing. These weren't idle doodles; they were portraits drawn with the skill of someone who had spent years perfecting their craft.

But I couldn't draw.

The further I flipped, the stranger the pages became. Some were filled with sprawling journal entries, words crammed into every inch of space, the handwriting growing jagged and uneven as though written in a feverish rush. Others held scrawled diagrams of mechanisms I couldn't begin to understand, lines and gears connecting in ways that hinted at a deeper purpose.

Then I found an entry that stopped me cold:

"Nikolai thinks he's in charge, but control is an illusion. Chaos will always find a way. That's where I come in."

The words made my stomach twist. Nikolai? Who was Nikolai? The tone of the entry wasn't reflective or questioning—it was assertive, almost mocking, as though the writer were addressing him directly.

I turned the page, searching for answers, but the questions only multiplied. More names appeared, scattered across the pages like breadcrumbs: **Silas, Ravenna, Noah, Elior, Selene & Isidore.** They weren't just names—they felt like voices, identities. The words carried a distinct rhythm for each one, as though they belonged to different people.

The Burden of Names

"**Ravenna** always wants to take the reins, but she doesn't see the bigger picture. It's not about balance; it's about survival."

"**Nikolai** is too soft. He doesn't understand what it takes to protect us. That's why I exist."

"**Noah**'s too quiet, but he sees more than he lets on. Don't underestimate him."

Each name felt heavier than the last, as though they were people I should have known but didn't. They didn't feel like characters in a story or placeholders for a math problem. They felt real.

I closed the notebook, my hands trembling. My mind raced, trying to make sense of what I had just seen. Was this some kind of elaborate joke? Had someone slipped the notebook into my bag to mess with me?

But that didn't explain the handwriting.

I knew it was mine.

I set the notebook on my desk, staring at it like it might spring to life. Part of me wanted to shove it back into the bag and forget I'd ever found it. Another part of me—a quieter, more insistent part—knew I couldn't.

The notebook wasn't just a curiosity. It was a warning.

Something was happening to me, something I didn't understand. And whatever it was, it wasn't going away.

The notebook wasn't just a glimpse into the unknown. It was a doorway. And once I'd opened it, there was no turning back.

The Night I Woke Up in the Park

The gaps in my memory were no longer just lapses. They had grown into something darker, something that loomed over every moment of my life. It wasn't just that I was losing time—I was losing control.

I realized this fully on a night I'll never forget, though the beginning of it is nothing but a void.

A Shiver in the Dark

When I opened my eyes, the first thing I felt was the cold. It gnawed at my skin, cutting through the thin fabric of my pajama top. I sat up, disoriented, as the world around me came into focus. I wasn't in my bed. I wasn't even in my house.

I was on a park bench, shivering beneath the faint glow of distant streetlights. Their hum buzzed in my ears, steady and ominous, like a warning I couldn't quite decipher.

I looked down at myself. My pajama bottoms were damp, clinging to my legs from the dew that blanketed the night. My feet were bare, the soles scraped and aching, as if I'd walked over gravel paths and hadn't stopped until I reached this bench.

I froze, my breath clouding in the chill air. My mind raced, desperate to make sense of what I was seeing. How had I gotten here? Why was I outside, miles from home, in the middle of the night?

The last thing I remembered was going to bed, exhausted from another grueling day of practice and training. I'd turned off my bedroom light, pulled the blanket over me, and closed my eyes, certain I would wake up to the blaring alarm clock the next morning.

But now? Now I was sitting in a park I barely recognized, alone, under a sky smeared with thin clouds and flickering stars.

The Walk Home

Panic set in quickly. I scrambled to my feet, the rough surface of the gravel path biting into my skin. Every sound seemed amplified in the stillness of the night—the rustling of leaves, the distant hum of cars, the soft creak of the bench as I moved.

I had to get home. That was my only thought.

But the walk home was a nightmare. The shadows stretched long and sharp, flickering under the streetlights like they were alive. The air felt heavier with every step, pressing in around me, making it hard to breathe. My heart pounded in my chest, each beat loud enough to echo in my ears.

What scared me most wasn't the dark streets or the strange stillness of the park. It was the absence in my mind—the gaping void where the memory of the last few hours should have been.

What had I done? Where had I been before I ended up on that bench? I searched my thoughts for answers, but there was nothing. No images, no fragments, no whispers. Just emptiness.

The House That Didn't Feel Safe

When I finally reached my house, it stood there in the darkness, silent and unwelcoming. For the first time, it didn't feel like a sanctuary. The familiar outline of the porch, the warm glow of the porch light, even the faint silhouette of my father's tennis rackets leaning against the wall—it all seemed foreign.

I crept inside, careful not to make a sound. My bare feet padded softly against the wooden floor as I locked the door behind me, the click of the deadbolt loud enough to make me flinch. I stood there for a moment, leaning against the door, trying to calm the tremor in my hands.

The house was still, the kind of silence that felt heavy and oppressive like it was waiting for something to break it. I tiptoed to my room, every creak of the floorboards sending a fresh jolt of panic through me.

Once inside, I locked my bedroom door and leaned against it, sliding down until I was sitting on the floor. My legs were trembling, and my breathing was shallow and uneven. The room was dark, but I didn't dare turn on the light.

The Fear That Stayed

I didn't sleep that night. How could I?

Every time I closed my eyes, I imagined waking up somewhere else—another park, an empty street, or worse, somewhere I wouldn't even recognize. The thought that I could lose myself so completely that I could go to sleep in my bed and wake up miles away was too much to bear.

I stayed on the floor, hugging my knees to my chest as the hours dragged by. The darkness felt like it was pressing in on me, wrapping around my mind like a suffocating blanket.

When the first light of dawn finally crept through the curtains, it brought no relief. The shadows on the walls receded, but the shadow in my mind remained. I wasn't just afraid of losing time anymore. I was afraid of myself—of what I might do, of where I might go, of what I might become.

That night wasn't the last time I woke up somewhere I didn't remember going. But it was the first, and it left a mark on me I'll never forget.

The Emergence of the Void

Over time, the fragments of my life began to align like the pieces of a puzzle I hadn't realized I was solving. The notebook, the memory gaps, the unexplainable episodes— all of it was leading to a revelation far larger than anything I could chalk up to stress or overwork.

My mind wasn't what I thought it was. It wasn't singular, cohesive, or whole. It was fracturing, creating spaces I hadn't invited or even noticed at first. And in those spaces, others began to emerge.

The Personas Take Shape

Each persona didn't just appear—they rose, like answers to questions I hadn't yet asked, responses to needs and challenges I couldn't handle alone. They weren't random; they had purpose, structure, and intent.

The first I came to recognize was **Silas**.

Silas was driven by wrath. His presence was undeniable, a force that surged through me in moments of anger or fear. He didn't just feel my rage—he wielded it, sharp and unyielding, as both a weapon and a shield. When I was cornered and powerless, Silas was the one who stepped forward, his intensity drowning out hesitation, doubt, or fear.

Then there was **Ravenna**, the artist.

Ravenna's energy was softer, though no less consuming. She emerged when emotions grew too large to contain, channeling them into vivid, breathtaking creations. The sketches in the notebook, the haunting lines of poetry—they were hers. Through her, feelings I couldn't face were transformed into art. Her work was raw, honest, and unnervingly beautiful, each stroke of the pen or brush speaking truths I hadn't been able to acknowledge.

Next came **Nikolai**, the organizer.

Nikolai was a control personified. Methodical and precise, he worked tirelessly to keep the others in check. His voice was calm, firm, and deliberate, always pushing for order amid the chaos. When Silas threatened to lash out, or Ravenna's emotions risked consuming everything, it was Nikolai who stepped in, organizing the mess into something manageable. But even he couldn't always hold the balance.

Then there was **Noah**, who I hadn't fully understood at first. Noah didn't charge forward like Silas or create like Ravenna. His presence was quiet, almost soothing, pulling me into moments of stillness when the chaos became too much. But that stillness had a weight to it, one that sometimes felt like drowning. Noah wasn't just resting—he was resignation, an escape from the pressure of being everything at once.

And still, there were more.

Elior whispered from the edges, a voice tinged with yearning and dissatisfaction, forever watching what others had and longing for it. **Selene** appeared in moments of indulgence, seeking solace in small comforts that rarely lasted. And finally, **Isidore**—calculated and ambitious—saw the world as a game to be won, a system to exploit for personal gain.

Not Just Fragments

They weren't just pieces of me, fractured and incomplete. They were distinct, fully formed identities, each with its own voice, its own perspective, its own role in my life.

Silas was rage.

Ravenna was expression.

Nikolai was order.

Noah was rest.

Elior was longing.

Selene was indulgence.

Isidore was ambition.

Each one served a purpose, stepping forward when the moment demanded it. Together, they made up what I came to call the void—not because it was empty, but because it was vast, a place within me that I couldn't fully comprehend.

Understanding the Void

At first, I feared them. How could I not? Their voices were louder than mine, and their actions were sometimes unpredictable and beyond my control. I felt like a passenger in my own mind, watching as they made choices I didn't understand left marks I couldn't erase.

But the more I listened, the more I began to see the truth. The void wasn't my enemy. It was a part of me, and so were they.

Silas wasn't just wrath; he was protection. Ravenna wasn't just art; she was catharsis. Nikolai wasn't just order; he was stability. Each of them rose to handle what I couldn't face alone.

They weren't my weakness. They were my strength.

The void wasn't just a fracture in my mind—it was a world unto itself. And in that world lived the many faces of me.

A Warning and a Promise

To my son: If you ever feel the stirrings of a Void within you, do not fear it. It will not mean you are broken or lost.

It will not mark the end of who you are. Instead, it will signal the beginning of something extraordinary—a journey unlike any other, one that only you can navigate.

The void is not your enemy, though at times it may feel like one. It is not a curse, though its weight may make it seem so. The void is a tool forged by your mind to protect, to create, to survive. But like any tool, its power depends on how you wield it. If left unchecked, it can consume you, pulling you into the chaos and darkness within. But if you choose to face it, to understand it, it can become your greatest ally, a wellspring of strength and insight.

A Legacy of Strength

When I first encountered my own void, I thought it would destroy me. I believed it was a sign of weakness, a flaw I needed to hide. It took me years to understand that it was neither. The void did not make me weak; it made me stronger, more adaptable, and more attuned to the complexities of life.

Through the void, I discovered parts of myself I didn't know existed—some fierce, some tender, all essential. It allowed me to endure when I thought I couldn't, to create when I felt empty, to fight when I was afraid. It shaped me into the person I am today.

This is the legacy I pass to you—not the void itself, but the strength to face it. The courage to listen to its voices without letting them drown you. The wisdom to find balance among its many pieces.

Closing Thought

This book is my attempt to guide you through that journey, should you ever need it. It is the map I didn't have when I stood at the edge of the void, uncertain and afraid. I want you to recognize the signs early—the subtle shifts in thought, the moments when you feel like someone else is looking out through your eyes. I want you to understand the pressures that can awaken the void, the challenges that might fracture your mind in ways you can't predict.

But more than anything, I want you to know that the void is not something to fear.

It is both a mystery and a gift, a space where the many facets of your being can exist and grow. It will not always be easy to navigate. There will be times when its pull feels too strong when the voices within it seem louder than your own. But its true power lies not in its existence but in your ability to master it—to turn its chaos into harmony, its shadows into light.

Let my story be your compass, as the void once was mine. Together, we will turn the chaos into clarity, the darkness into light, and the many faces of you into a unified whole.

This is my promise to you: You are not broken. You are not alone. You are extraordinary.

Chapter 2: The Seven Sins, Seven Personas

The Seven Sins, Seven Personas

"In the depths of the Void, they revealed themselves—not as strangers, but as facets of me, each with a name, a voice, and a purpose."

When I first began to understand the void, it wasn't an easy revelation. What felt like chaos slowly began to take shape. The voices that whispered in my mind, the urges that pulled me in different directions, were not random—they were personas, manifestations of my mind's attempt to navigate a world that often felt overwhelming.

Each persona had a distinct personality, abilities, a name, and a role. They were neither entirely good nor entirely bad, but each carried both a gift and a burden. They were born from the Seven Deadly Sins, but over time, I came to see them as more than just shadows of vice—they were reflections of human nature, with all its complexities.

Silas: Wrath – The Warrior

"The protector who fights with unrelenting fury to safeguard what matters most."

Silas is not a presence you can ignore. When he takes control, it is as if the world narrows into a single, uncompromising purpose: protect, defend, and survive. He is Wrath personified, but not the reckless anger of someone losing control. Silas is precise, calculated, and focused like a predator locking onto its prey. His strength doesn't come from rage alone—it comes from a profound instinct to protect, no matter the cost.

The Awakening of Wrath

I first felt Silas's presence when I was 14. It was after school, in the dusty corner of the playground, where bullies loved to lurk. I had been cornered by four older boys, their sneers and mocking laughter reverberating through the still air. My heart pounded with fear as they pushed me around, their taunts growing sharper, more invasive.

And then, it happened. It was as if something deep inside me snapped. Fear turned into heat, a blazing fire that coursed through my veins. My vision narrowed, the world around me blurring into insignificance. I didn't hear their laughter anymore; didn't feel the sting of their words. When I came back to myself, I was in the principal's office. Two of the boys were in the nurse's care—one nursing a broken nose, the other a fractured arm. My knuckles were raw, bruised, and aching.

The principal's words were a blur as he berated me for my "violent outburst." I couldn't explain what had happened—I didn't even remember throwing a punch. All I knew was that I had felt a force take over, a force that wouldn't let me be afraid. That force was Silas, the warrior within.

The Protector in Action

Silas emerges in moments of crisis, his presence as undeniable as the storm clouds before a hurricane. Once, during a late-night walk home, I felt the prickling sense of being followed. The shadowed figure behind me quickened its pace, closing the gap. Panic bubbled in my chest, but before it could take hold, Silas surged forward.

I turned to face the threat, my body moving before my mind could catch up. My fists clenched, my stance instinctively defensive. The stranger lunged, but Silas was faster. Within seconds, the man was disarmed and on the ground, stunned and reeling. I didn't stay to reflect or process—I ran, my heart pounding with the aftermath. It wasn't until I was safe that I realized what had happened.

Silas's precision is unmatched. In moments of danger, he assesses threats with lightning speed, responding with an efficiency that borders on superhuman. He doesn't hesitate, doesn't deliberate—he acts.

The Consequences of Fury

But Silas's power comes with a cost. His focus on the immediate threat blinds him to the long-term consequences of his actions. His strength, while protective, can also be destructive.

There was a time when Silas emerged during an argument with a close friend. The disagreement started small but escalated quickly, my friend's words striking a nerve I hadn't realized was raw. Silas didn't just defend me—he attacked. My voice, usually measured, became sharp and cutting, each word like a blade. When the argument ended, my friend walked away, hurt and distant. Though I had "won" the fight, the relationship was irreparably damaged.

Silas's presence also takes a physical toll. After he retreats, I am left drained, my muscles aching as if I've just run a marathon. The adrenaline rush leaves behind a hollow exhaustion that lingers for days.

Learning to Wield the Fire

Silas is a fire—intense, protective, but dangerously consuming if left unchecked. For years, I feared his presence, seeing him as a force I couldn't control. But as I grew older, I began to understand that Silas wasn't my enemy. He was a part of me, a necessary force that had to be guided, not suppressed.

I've learned to channel Silas's energy into constructive outlets. Martial arts became a refuge, a place where his raw intensity could be focused and refined. The discipline of training taught me how to let Silas take the light without losing myself to him. Physical workouts became a way to release the pressure he carried, transforming his fury into strength.

A Message to My Son

To my son: If you ever feel Silas stirring within you, do not fear him. He is not here to harm you—he is here to protect you. Silas is a gift, a reminder that strength is not just about power but about purpose. But remember, his fire must be wielded with wisdom.

Let Silas teach you courage in the face of fear and resilience in the face of adversity. But never let him rule you. Learn to guide him, to channel his energy into actions that build rather than destroy. Strength without control is a wildfire, but strength with discipline is an unbreakable shield. Silas is your protector, your warrior, your fire. Use him well.

Ravenna: Lust – The Artist

"The passionate artist who channels emotions into beauty and self-expression."

Ravenna is the siren within me, the voice that calls to the soul and turns emotion into art. She is Lust, but her desire goes far beyond the physical. Ravenna craves connection—emotional, intellectual, and spiritual. She lives for beauty in its rawest, most vulnerable form and seeks to express it in ways that linger long after the moment has passed.

When Ravenna takes the light, the world transforms. Colors deepen, music resonates with haunting clarity, and even the smallest details—an old book's frayed edges, the flicker of candlelight—feel like treasures waiting to be captured. She doesn't just see the world; she feels it, absorbing its beauty and pain with an intensity that can be both inspiring and overwhelming.

The Creative Spark

Ravenna's influence is undeniable in my creative pursuits. She is the reason I can lose myself in the flow of artistic expression, why I can sit on a canvas for hours without noticing the passage of time. Her touch is in every poem I've written every painting I've poured my soul into.

There was a time when I didn't understand the power of Ravenna's presence. I was 16, struggling to articulate the feelings of longing and heartbreak that had consumed me after my first real crush ended in rejection. Words seemed inadequate, and I felt lost, unable to express the ache in my chest. That was when Ravenna stepped in.

One evening, I found myself sketching aimlessly at my desk, the movements of my hand guided by something beyond conscious thought. When I finally looked down, the page was filled with the beginnings of a portrait—an abstract depiction of vulnerability and desire. Over the next week, the sketch grew into a painting, layers of color and texture building a story of longing and hope.

When I finished, I stared at the canvas and realized it wasn't just a representation of my feelings—it was a catharsis, a release. Ravenna had turned my pain into something beautiful, something that gave me clarity and peace.

The Allure of Connection

Ravenna doesn't just crave beauty; she craves connection. Her desire for intimacy and understanding pushes me to open up to others and seek out relationships that transcend the superficial. She is the reason I've had moments of profound closeness with friends and loved ones, moments where walls fell away, and the truth was laid bare.

But her longing can also leave me vulnerable. There have been times when Ravenna's intensity has driven me to over-invest in relationships, pouring my energy into people who couldn't or wouldn't reciprocate. In one instance, I found myself chasing the attention of someone who saw me as little more than a passing curiosity. Ravenna's need for connection blinded me to the reality of the situation, leaving me heartbroken when the relationship inevitably fell apart.

The Fragility of Passion

Ravenna's greatest strength is also her greatest weakness. Her passion allows her to create beauty from chaos, but it also leaves her—and me—exposed. The depth of her emotions can be overwhelming, turning small disappointments into crushing blows.

I remember one particularly vivid moment when Ravenna's vulnerability overtook me. I had been working on a painting for weeks, pouring every ounce of emotion into it. When I finally unveiled it to a group of friends, their reactions were polite but indifferent. They didn't see what I saw, didn't feel what I felt. Ravenna's heart broke at that moment, and mine did, too. The rejection, though unintentional, felt personal, as though my very soul had been dismissed.

The Muse and the Mirror

Ravenna is both a muse and a mirror. She inspires creativity, pushing me to explore the depths of my emotions and turn them into something tangible. But she also forces me to confront the fragility of the human experience to acknowledge that beauty and pain are often intertwined.

She reminds me that to create is to feel deeply and to feel deeply is to take a risk. Not every poem will resonate, not every painting will be understood, and not every connection will last. But that doesn't make the effort any less worthwhile.

A Message to My Son

To my son: If you ever feel Ravenna stirring within you, let her guide you, but do so with caution. Her passion is a gift, a force that can transform the mundane into the extraordinary. She will show you the world's beauty in ways you never thought possible, and she will help you express the feelings you cannot put into words.

But remember, Ravenna's intensity is not without its price. Her desire for connection can leave you vulnerable, and her passion can consume you if you let it. Learn to balance her gifts with wisdom. Create, but don't lose yourself in the process. Seek connection, but know when to walk away.

Ravenna is your muse, your artist, your mirror. She will teach you to see the world not just as it is but as it could be. Embrace her gifts, but never forget that even the brightest flame needs to be tempered. Let her guide you toward beauty, but never at the cost of your own light.

Nikolai: Pride – The Leader

"The leader who balances the collective, wielding confidence as both shield and sword to bring order to the chaos."

Nikolai stands tall at the heart of the void, the unyielding figure who ensures order amidst the tumult of clashing voices and emotions. He is Pride, but not the kind that blinds or corrodes. Nikolai's pride is refined, a quiet assurance born of capability and composure. He is the embodiment of control, the conductor who harmonizes the cacophony of personas, turning chaos into a symphony.

For much of my life, Nikolai has been the face that others recognize as "me." Polished, articulate, and dependable, he carries the weight of societal expectations without flinching. He is the one who projects an unshakeable confidence even when doubt gnaws at the edges of my mind. Yet, beneath his poised exterior lies the constant tension of his role—the gatekeeper who must decide which persona steps into the light and when all while carrying the burden of their collective existence.

The Polished Facade

Nikolai's presence is unmistakable. When he takes charge, the whirlwind of emotions and impulses quiets, and everything sharpens into focus. He thrives in situations that demand composure and decisiveness, excelling in environments where others might falter under pressure.

I remember one particular moment during my teenage years when Nikolai's influence was pivotal. It was the finals of a regional math Olympiad, and the stakes were immense. The room was silent, save for the scratch of pencils and the occasional cough, as dozens of competitors wrestled with problems designed to push us to our mental limits.

As I stared at the paper, panic began to creep in. The equations felt alien, the numbers blurring together. But then, Nikolai emerged. He silenced the noise in my head, bringing clarity and focus. Each problem became a puzzle, each equation a challenge to conquer. With unwavering confidence, he guided my hand, solving the questions with precision and speed.

When the results were announced, and my name was called the winner, I felt an overwhelming sense of pride—not just for myself but for the collective effort of the void. Yet, even in that moment of triumph, Nikolai's gaze turned inward. He knew the victory was not his alone. Somewhere in the shadows, Greed had been calculating the stakes, and Envy had been whispering reminders of the competitors to surpass.

The Gatekeeper's Burden

Nikolai's role extends beyond external accomplishments; he is the internal gatekeeper, the one who keeps the void from descending into anarchy. He evaluates every situation with strategic precision, determining which persona's strengths are most needed. Whether it's channeling **Ravenna**'s creative spark, leaning into **Silas**'s protective fury, or harnessing **Isidore**'s meticulous planning, Nikolai ensures that the right voice is heard at the right time.

This control, however, comes at a cost. The weight of leadership often leaves Nikolai isolated, unable to show vulnerability even when the burden becomes too much to bear. I recall a time during college when this isolation reached its peak.

As president of a student organization, I was responsible for managing events, mediating conflicts, and maintaining the group's reputation. To everyone else, I was the epitome of confidence and competence. But behind closed doors, the pressure mounted. Deadlines loomed, interpersonal dynamics grew tense, and the line between "me" and the personas blurred.

One evening, after a particularly challenging day, I stood in front of a mirror, staring at my reflection. The face that looked back was Nikolai's—calm, composed, but distant. It felt like a mask, one I couldn't remove. I whispered, "Who am I without this? And what happens if I fail?" The silence that followed was deafening.

The Cracks in the Armor

For all his strengths, Nikolai is not invincible. His pride, while a source of resilience, can also become a barrier. His need for control often prevents him from sharing the weight of responsibility, leaving him to bear burdens that might otherwise be lightened through collaboration.

There was a time in my early twenties when this need for control led to a breakdown. Working a high-stakes corporate job, I juggled deadlines, client expectations, and a relentless workload. Nikolai thrived in the chaos, organizing every task with military precision. But as the weeks turned into months, the cracks began to show.

One evening, after yet another late night at the office, a small oversight—a missed email—triggered a chain reaction of frustration and self-doubt. For a moment, Nikolai faltered. The carefully constructed walls of his composure crumbled, and Thomas surged forward.

I don't remember much of what happened next, but when I came back to myself, my desk was in disarray, papers scattered and torn. My knuckles throbbed from punching the wall, and the accusatory silence of my coworkers the next day was a reminder of the consequences. It was a stark lesson: even the strongest leaders must learn to acknowledge their limits.

A Beacon of Order

Nikolai remains the anchor of the void, the persona that ensures the others do not spiral out of control. He is not perfect, but his imperfections make him human. He is a reminder that leadership is not about infallibility—it's about balance, about guiding the chaos without suppressing it.

To my son: If you inherit this gift, know that Nikolai's strength lies not just in his ability to lead but in his willingness to listen. He will teach you that confidence is not about always being right—it's about knowing when to stand firm and when to adapt. He is your shield and your sword, your lighthouse in the storm.

Remember, leadership is not about silencing the void—it's about learning to navigate its depths with courage and compassion. Nikolai will show you the way, but it is up to you to follow. Together, you can transform the chaos into something extraordinary.

A Message to My Son

To my son: If you ever feel the burden of leadership pressing down on your shoulders, remember this—true strength lies not in never faltering but in how you rise when you do. Nikolai will teach you to stand firm, face challenges with unwavering confidence, and guide the voices within toward harmony.

But know this: leadership is not about control—it's about balance. It's about listening to the voices within, even the ones that challenge you, and finding a way to bring them together. Nikolai will remind you that pride is not a sin when it comes from a place of self-belief and respect for others.

You may feel alone at times, as Nikolai often does, but you are never truly alone. You carry within you a symphony of strengths waiting to be orchestrated. Trust in yourself, trust in Nikolai, and know that even in your darkest moments, you have the power to bring light to the chaos.

Elior: Envy – The Competitor

"The relentless competitor who thrives on ambition and the pursuit of greatness."

Elior—his name itself feels sharp, like the edge of a blade forged in the fires of ambition. He is the part of me that refuses to settle, that looks at the achievements of others and whispers, *You can do better.* Unlike the mindless envy that corrodes and destroys, Elior's envy is a force of propulsion, pushing me toward goals I once thought unattainable. When Elior takes the light, the world narrows into a singular focus, every distraction falling away until all that remains is the finish line.

The Relentless Drive for Excellence

Elior's influence often manifests in moments of competition, where the stakes are high, and the room for error is slim. I remember one particular math Olympiad that stretched my abilities to their very limits. The competition was fierce, the problems brutal, and the air in the room crackled with tension.

As the timer began, I felt a familiar shift. My hands steadied, my breathing slowed, and my thoughts became razor-sharp. Elior had stepped forward, his voice clear and commanding in my mind.

"Focus. Don't let them get ahead. Every move matters."

I worked through the problems with a precision that felt almost mechanical, breaking each one down into manageable parts. Elior didn't just solve the equations—he studied the competitors, analyzing their pacing, gauging their reactions, and calculating exactly how much time I could afford to spend on each question. By the end of the competition, I had not only finished but done so with clarity and confidence that stunned my peers.

Later, as I stood on the podium accepting my award, I could feel Elior's pride mingled with my own. But beneath that pride was a whisper of discontent: *This isn't enough. You can do more.*

The Shadows of Comparison

Elior's greatest strength is also his greatest weakness. His drive for excellence often blinds me to the value of balance and perspective. Under his influence, success becomes an obsession, and every achievement is measured against the accomplishments of others.

There was a time in high school when I was locked in an unspoken rivalry with another student, a brilliant and charismatic boy named Ethan. He was everything I wanted to be—top of the class, captain of the debate team, and the kind of person who could light up a room with his presence.

Elior saw Ethan not as a friend but as a benchmark, a living reminder of where I fell short. Every interaction with him became a battle in my mind, and every shared classroom was a silent arena. When Ethan scored higher than me on a physics exam, Elior was relentless, driving me to study late into the night, fueled by a mix of envy and determination.

While my grades improved, my health and relationships suffered. I became irritable, distant, and consumed by a need to prove myself. By the time I surpassed Ethan in academic rankings, the victory felt hollow. Elior's voice, once so empowering, had turned critical: *Why did it take so long? Why aren't you further ahead?*

The Cost of Ambition

Elior's pursuit of greatness often comes at a price. His influence has driven me to sleepless nights, strained friendships, and moments of deep self-doubt. His relentless comparisons, while motivating, can also strip away the joy of success, replacing it with a constant sense of inadequacy.

One night, after an especially grueling week of tennis practice and exam prep, I found myself sitting alone in my room, surrounded by trophies and certificates. They should have felt like accomplishments, symbols of hard work and perseverance. Instead, they felt like hollow reminders of all the ways I still fell short.

Elior's voice echoed in my mind, urging me to keep pushing, to never stop striving. But at that moment, I realized that his ambition, unchecked, was leading me down a path of isolation and burnout.

Harnessing Elior's Ambition

To truly benefit from Elior's gifts, I've had to learn how to temper his relentless drive with balance and self-compassion. It's not easy—Elior's voice is persuasive, his demands urgent—but I've found ways to channel his energy constructively.

For instance, I've started setting boundaries around my goals, defining not just what I want to achieve but also why it matters. I've also begun celebrating small victories, even when Elior insists they're not enough. Most importantly, I've learned to recognize when his comparisons are fueling growth and when they're eroding my sense of self-worth.

A Message to My Son

To my son: If you feel the stirrings of Elior within you, embrace his ambition, but do so with care. Let his drive push you to excel, but never let it consume you. Remember that success is not defined by how you measure up to others but by how you grow and evolve as an individual.

Elior's gift is the ability to see the potential to strive for greatness. Use that gift wisely. Celebrate your achievements, no matter how small, and remember that you are enough, even when the world—or Elior—tells you otherwise. Ambition is a powerful tool, but it must always be wielded with purpose and balance.

Noah: Sloth – The Observer

"The quiet observer who offers clarity through stillness and reflection."

Noah—what a fitting name for the calm amidst the storm. He is the persona who waits, watches and absorbs the chaos that surrounds him without yielding to it. Unlike Silas, whose presence roars like a wildfire, or Ravenna, whose passion dances like an uncontainable flame, Noah is the stillness, the slow breath in a whirlwind of chaos. He doesn't speak often, nor does he act rashly. When Noah takes the light, life feels as though it is being viewed through a lens of quiet clarity. Every movement becomes deliberate, every thought deliberate, and every word measured.

The World in Stillness

Noah's influence began to emerge during moments of exhaustion—times when the relentless pace of my life seemed unbearable. I first noticed his presence during a particularly grueling week in high school. Between late-night math drills, an important tennis tournament, and escalating drama with my friends, I found myself running on empty. My mind felt like a rubber band stretched too thin, ready to snap at any moment.

One Friday evening, after another long day, I walked into my room, collapsed onto the bed, and closed my eyes. I expected my thoughts to race as usual, darting between the day's events and the challenges ahead. But instead, everything grew quiet. It was a profound, eerie silence, as though someone had turned the volume down on my world.

I opened my eyes, and everything felt different. The cluttered desk that usually overwhelmed me seemed insignificant. The noise of the television in the next room faded into a distant hum. For the first time in what felt like forever, my mind wasn't a battleground. It was Noah—his presence like a deep, calming breath. He didn't push me to act or think; he simply let me *be*.

The Wisdom of Detachment

Noah's strength lies in his ability to detach and observe. While the other personas tend to take action—whether through Silas's force or Nikolai's control—Noah prefers to step back, giving me the gift of perspective. Once, during a heated argument between my parents and me about my future, Noah's influence saved me from a spiral of anger and frustration.

My father was adamant that I focus solely on tennis, believing it was my ticket to college and success. My mother wanted me to prioritize academics, pushing me toward medicine. I felt caught between their expectations, my own desires muffled by the noise of their conflicting demands. As their voices grew louder, I felt the familiar surge of Silas's anger bubbling within me. But before it could take over, a wave of calm swept through me.

Noah had taken the light. He silenced the noise in my head and allowed me to hear my parents—not just their words but their intentions and fears. For the first time, I truly *listened*, and in that stillness, I realized they weren't trying to control me. They were trying to protect me in the only ways they knew how.

I didn't say much during that argument. Noah didn't believe in speaking unless it was necessary. But when I finally responded, my words were measured, deliberate, and calm. It wasn't a solution, but it was the first time we had a conversation rather than a shouting match. That moment of clarity was a gift only Noah could give.

The Shadows of Inaction

However, Noah's stillness is a double-edged sword. His detachment, while insightful, can sometimes leave me paralyzed. There have been moments when his reluctance to act has cost me dearly.

I remember a time in college when I was supposed to attend an important interview for an internship. The opportunity was a dream come true—working with a top-tier firm that could open doors for my future. But on the morning of the interview, as I sat at my desk rehearsing my answers, Noah's influence crept in.

Instead of feeling anxious or excited, I felt detached, as though the outcome didn't matter. The clock ticked away, and I remained frozen, analyzing every possible scenario. Should I go and risk failing? Should I call and reschedule? Should I even pursue this path at all? By the time I finally decided to leave, the opportunity had passed. The interview slot was gone, and with it, a chance I had worked so hard to secure.

Noah's stillness, while valuable, can sometimes border on stagnation. His preference for observation over participation makes him the hardest persona to reconcile. While his insights are profound, his inability—or unwillingness—to act often leaves me grappling with regret.

Finding Balance in Stillness

Noah's lessons are among the most difficult to embrace. He teaches me the value of stepping back and finding clarity in the chaos. But he also reminds me that observation is only the first step. To truly grow, I must use his wisdom to guide my actions and turn insight into impact.

A Message to My Son

To my son: If you ever feel the pull of Noah's stillness, embrace it. Let his calm wash over you and quiet the storm within. But don't let him hold you in place. Noah is a guide, not a jailer. His gift is perspective, and it is up to you to use that perspective to move forward.

Remember, the world is not a race to be won or a problem to be solved. It is a story to be lived. And sometimes, the best way to find your next step is to stop, breathe, and let the quiet show you the way.

Selene: Gluttony – The Nurturer

"The warm nurturer who finds joy in comfort and connection through indulgence."

Selene is the embodiment of warmth and solace, a persona whose very presence feels like a comforting embrace on a cold, weary day. She is Gluttony, not in the destructive sense of excess, but as the nurturer who understands the importance of finding joy in life's pleasures. When Selene takes the light, the world softens. Stresses fade into the background, and every sensation feels heightened—every flavor more vivid, every touch more soothing, every moment a small piece of bliss.

The Nurturer's Touch

Selene often emerges during times of exhaustion or emotional strain. When the relentless demands of life leave me drained, it is Selene who steps forward, offering comfort in ways I didn't even know I needed.

I remember one particularly brutal stretch during my final year of high school. Between preparing for college entrance exams, managing tennis tournaments, and navigating the complexities of friendships and budding romances, I felt like I was running on fumes. One night, after collapsing onto the couch with an untouched dinner plate beside me, I felt a shift.

Selene took the light, and everything changed. My focus turned away from the pile of textbooks on the desk and toward the simple joys I had been neglecting. I found myself in the kitchen, cooking a dish from scratch—something warm and savory, with spices that filled the air with an almost magical aroma. She made me savor every bite, each mouthful a reminder of the care I owed myself. Later, wrapped in a blanket and watching a movie I hadn't seen since childhood, I felt a sense of peace I hadn't experienced in weeks.

Selene's gift is her ability to nurture and heal the parts of me that are frayed and worn by reminding me that it's okay to pause and indulge in life's small comforts.

The Allure of Indulgence

However, Selene's nurturing nature can sometimes lead to overindulgence. Her voice, so soothing and persuasive, can tempt me into excess when I'm not careful. During college, there was a time when Selene's influence tipped the balance too far. It started innocently enough—a few nights of takeout after long study sessions, a glass of wine to unwind after a stressful day, and an extra hour of sleep on a Saturday morning.

Before I knew it, those small indulgences had become habits. My once-disciplined routine unraveled as Selene urged me to prioritize comfort over responsibility. Missed classes, skipped workouts, and a growing pile of uncompleted assignments became the norm. I justified it all with Selene's whispers: *You deserve this. You've been working so hard.*

It wasn't until I found myself struggling to catch up, staring at a report due in hours with a sinking feeling of dread, that I realized Selene's comfort had become a crutch. Her nurturing had shielded me from stress, yes, but it had also allowed me to avoid confronting the deeper issues I needed to address.

Finding Balance

Selene's influence has taught me that comfort is essential, but it must always be balanced with discipline and self-awareness. Her nurturing is a gift, but it can only be fully appreciated when paired with the resolve to face life's challenges head-on.

Over time, I've learned how to channel Selene's warmth constructively. I've developed rituals of self-care that honor her influence without letting it take over. I journal with a cup of tea on a quiet morning, cook meals that nourish both body and soul, and set aside time for rest after a productive day. All these are ways I've embraced Selene's presence while maintaining control.

The Strength in Vulnerability

One of Selene's most profound lessons is the importance of vulnerability. She reminds me that strength isn't always about pushing through adversity—it's also about recognizing when you need to step back and recharge.

During a particularly challenging time in my adult life, when career pressures and personal struggles left me feeling completely overwhelmed, it was Selene who helped me find a way forward. Instead of running myself into the ground trying to keep up with impossible expectations, I allowed myself to pause. I spent a weekend disconnected from work, surrounded by friends and family, savoring good food, laughter, and the simple comfort of connection.

When I returned to the challenges before me, I felt rejuvenated, ready to tackle them with clarity and energy I hadn't felt in months. Selene had shown me that sometimes, the greatest act of strength is admitting that you need a moment to breathe.

A Message to My Son

To my son: If you ever feel the pull of Selene within you, know that her gifts are invaluable. She will teach you the importance of self-care, the beauty of indulgence, and the healing power of connection. But remember, her comfort is not a destination—it is a resting place, a moment to gather strength before moving forward.

Selene will remind you to savor life's pleasures, but it is your responsibility to ensure that her warmth does not become a cocoon that shields you from growth. Embrace her gift, but pair it with discipline and purpose. In doing so, you will find not just comfort but resilience—the ability to face the world with both strength and grace.

Isidore: Greed – The Strategist

"The strategist who accumulates resources and prepares for every eventuality."

Isidore is the meticulous tactician, a persona whose influence is felt in every carefully crafted plan, every calculated decision, and every safeguard I've put in place. He embodies Greed, but his focus isn't on material possessions or wealth—it's on knowledge, preparation, and control. When Isidore takes the light, the world transforms into a chessboard, with every moving part of a larger strategy and every outcome a puzzle waiting to be solved.

The Mastermind

Isidore thrives in situations that require foresight and precision. His attention to detail is uncanny, bordering on obsession, and his ability to anticipate outcomes makes him invaluable in moments of uncertainty. I remember one instance during a pivotal academic competition. The final round was a timed event, with each team tasked to solve a series of complex mathematical problems under intense pressure. The room buzzed with tension. Competitors hunched over their desks, scratching out calculations and wiping sweat from their brows.

When my turn came, Isidore took the light. My mind sharpened, each problem breaking down into manageable parts. It was as if I could see not just the solution but the pathway to it, every variable falling into place with machine-like efficiency. While others faltered, second-guessing themselves, I moved with confidence, completing the task faster than anyone else in the room. My team won the event, and while others congratulated me on my "genius," I knew it wasn't entirely me. It was Isidore, orchestrating every move with unyielding focus.

The Planner and the Paradox

Isidore's gift is his unparalleled ability to plan and prepare. Whether it's managing finances, organizing an event, or navigating a personal crisis, his influence ensures that no detail is overlooked. He is the one who double-checks itineraries, researches every option, and creates backup plans for backup plans.

However, Isidore's meticulous nature often becomes a double-edged sword. His relentless drive for perfection can lead to overthinking and paralysis by analysis. During one particularly stressful period, I was tasked with presenting a major project at work. Isidore took over, ensuring every slide, every word, and every detail of the presentation was flawless. But his obsession didn't stop there—he continued tweaking and revising until the last minute, leaving me sleep-deprived and anxious. The presentation was a success, but the toll it took on my mental and physical health was undeniable.

A Moment of Crisis

There was another time when Isidore's influence saved me in a moment of real danger. Late one night, while driving home from a friend's house, I noticed another car tailgating me aggressively. The driver honked, swerved, and eventually sped ahead, only to cut me off and force me to a stop. Fear gripped me, but before panic could set in, Isidore emerged.

With a calmness that felt almost unnatural, I assessed the situation. Isidore noted the exits, calculated the distance to the nearest populated area, and recalled the self-defense tips I had once read in an article. I maneuvered the car with precision, taking a sudden turn onto a well-lit road where people were still milling about. The tailgater gave up, speeding off into the night. When I finally stopped to catch my breath, the memory of how I had reacted was hazy and fragmented—but the lingering sense of safety was proof of Isidore's intervention.

The Weight of Control

Isidore's greatest strength is his need for control, but it is also his greatest burden. His constant vigilance and relentless pursuit of readiness can be exhausting. There are nights when I lie awake, my mind racing with contingency plans and "what if" scenarios that may never come to pass. Isidore whispers in my ear, insisting that if I just think a little harder and plan a little better, I can avoid every failure and every misstep.

This need for control has strained relationships, as Isidore's presence often makes me seem distant or unyielding. Friends and family sometimes describe me as "cold" or "calculating," not realizing that beneath the surface lies a persona driven by the fear of failure, of being caught off guard.

The Rules of Engagement

Isidore's role within the dynamic of my personas is critical, but it is also one of the most tightly regulated. Under Larry's leadership, Isidore acts as the strategist, contributing his skills without overwhelming the system. However, in moments of extreme stress, Isidore can bypass this structure, taking control autonomously.

For example, during an intense argument with a colleague, Isidore's calculating nature took over. Rather than reacting emotionally, he dissected the argument, using logic and precision to dismantle the other person's points. While the confrontation ended in my favor, it left an uneasy tension that lingered long after the conversation was over.

When Larry maintains control, Isidore's contributions are invaluable. He ensures that the collective memory remains intact, that plans are executed smoothly, and that resources are allocated efficiently. But when Isidore acts independently, his focus on preparation and control can create dissonance, leaving me with fragmented memories and a sense of detachment.

A Message to My Son

To my son: If you ever feel the presence of Isidore within you, know that his gifts are immense. He will teach you the value of preparation, the importance of strategy, and the power of foresight. But remember, his strengths must be balanced with trust—trust in yourself, in others, and in the unpredictable nature of life.

Isidore will push you to be ready for anything, but life is not a puzzle that can always be solved in advance. Embrace his guidance, but do not let his need for control rob you of the joy of spontaneity and the lessons that come from imperfection. Preparation is important, but so is living in the moment. In this balance lies the true power of Isidore's gift.

Chapter 3: Is It in Our Blood?

Is It in Our Blood?

"The shadows of our past often stretch into the future, but understanding them can transform a curse into a gift."

From the moment I understood the complexity of my mind, a question haunted me: is this something I inherited? Could the void that shaped my life also find its way into yours, my son? As I learned to navigate my fragmented self, I began to wonder if Dissociative Identity Disorder (DID) might not just be a product of trauma but perhaps a thread woven into our very DNA. This chapter dives deep into that possibility, exploring how this unique condition might transcend generations, the early signs to watch for, and how to approach it as a gift rather than a burden.

The Mystery of Inheritance

Science has yet to definitively classify DID as a genetic disorder, but mental health conditions often have a hereditary component. Traits like heightened sensitivity, emotional intensity, and even a predisposition to dissociative tendencies can run through families. These aren't always negative traits; they often come with unique strengths, like creativity, problem-solving, and resilience. However, without proper guidance, they can spiral into challenges, as they did for me during my adolescence.

When I reflect on my own upbringing, I can't help but notice certain patterns in my family. My father, though never diagnosed, often displayed behaviors that seemed contradictory—one moment nurturing and patient, the next distant and unyielding. My mother, too, had moments of detachment, as if her mind had drifted elsewhere. They never spoke of these tendencies, and as a child, I didn't question them. But as I grew older and began to understand my own mind, I wondered if their fragmented behaviors were more than just quirks—if they were clues to an inherited predisposition.

The possibility of inheritance isn't just about passing down a disorder; it's about passing down a way of perceiving the world. A fragmented perspective might seem like a disadvantage, but it also allows for adaptability, creativity, and resilience. If this is in our blood, it means you might inherit not just the challenges but also the strengths that come with it.

The Early Signs

If DID has a hereditary aspect, then recognizing the early signs is critical—especially during adolescence, when identity begins to take shape. Looking back, the signs in me were subtle at first, like whispers in the wind, easy to dismiss as normal teenage behavior. But over time, they became impossible to ignore.

One of the first signs I noticed was the frequent memory lapses. At 14, I would find myself forgetting entire chunks of my day. I'd walk into the house with no recollection of my tennis practice or the grueling hours spent preparing for an upcoming Math Olympiad competition. My friends would joke about something funny I'd said in class, and I'd laugh along, pretending to remember. These weren't just forgetful moments—they were voids as if someone else had lived those hours for me.

Then came the conflicting interests. I was a dedicated athlete known for my discipline and drive. But suddenly, I began discovering poetry scrawled in notebooks I didn't recognize as my own or half-finished sketches of landscapes and faces I didn't recall creating. At one point, I even found a journal filled with detailed chess strategies, written in my handwriting but entirely foreign to my usual thought patterns. It was as though new pieces of myself were emerging, parts I hadn't met before.

My moods also became unpredictable. There were days when I was confident and outgoing, seamlessly navigating social interactions. On other days, I felt an overwhelming need to retreat, consumed by introspection or anxiety. This emotional inconsistency wasn't just teenage angst—it was the personas within me, each taking turns to step into the light.

Generational Echoes

If DID has a genetic component, its manifestation can vary greatly across generations. In me, it began with memory gaps and the emergence of distinct personas, each with its own skills and motivations. Silas, driven by wrath, emerged to protect me when I felt threatened. Ravenna awakened my creativity and passion, transforming the mundane into something extraordinary. And Nikolai became the leader, ensuring the chaos within didn't spiral out of control.

But in you, my son, it might look different. It could appear as a heightened sensitivity to emotions, a deep connection to creativity, or an uncanny ability to adapt to changing circumstances.

Understanding this condition as a spectrum rather than a fixed disorder is crucial. Not everyone with dissociative tendencies will develop distinct personas. For some, it may manifest as a heightened capacity for compartmentalization —an ability to separate emotions or experiences in ways that allow for incredible focus and resilience. For others, it might appear as a natural inclination toward empathy, creativity, or problem-solving.

This spectrum is why early recognition is so important. By identifying the signs, we can guide the condition toward becoming a strength rather than a weakness. This doesn't mean suppressing the personas or forcing them into conformity—it means understanding them, nurturing their unique gifts, and ensuring they don't consume you.

The Adolescent Crucible

Adolescence is a critical period for anyone, but for those with a predisposition to DID, it's a time of heightened vulnerability. The pressures of identity formation, social expectations, and academic demands can amplify dissociative tendencies. For me, it was a perfect storm.

At 14, I was navigating the relentless demands of tennis training, academic excellence, and extracurricular commitments like the Math Olympiad. My father's high expectations only added to the pressure, as he pushed me to excel in sports while my teachers urged me to focus on academics. My friends, meanwhile, expected me to maintain the confident, carefree persona they had come to rely on. This constant juggling act left little room for vulnerability, and so my mind did what it needed to survive—it fractured.

Each persona that emerged during this time was a response to these pressures. Nikolai took control during moments of high stakes, ensuring I performed at my best. Selene, my nurturing presence, sought solace in indulgence when the pressure became too much. And Silas emerged during moments of conflict, ready to protect me at all costs. These personas weren't just coping mechanisms—they were lifelines, each offering a unique form of strength.

Recognizing the Void in You

To my son, if you ever notice similar patterns in yourself—memory lapses, conflicting interests, or mood swings that feel out of your control—don't ignore them. These signs don't mean you are broken; they mean your mind is finding its own way to adapt and thrive. The key is to pay attention, to observe without judgment, and to seek understanding.

Ask yourself:

- Are there moments when you feel like someone else is in control?
- Do you find yourself drawn to new hobbies or skills seemingly out of nowhere?
- Are there gaps in your memory, or do you feel detached from certain experiences?

These questions aren't meant to scare you—they're meant to guide you. The earlier you recognize these tendencies, the more power you have to shape them into something positive.

The Gift Within the Void

It's easy to see DID as a curse, especially in its early stages when confusion and fear dominate. But as I've learned, it's also a gift. The ability to compartmentalize, to shift perspectives, and to tap into distinct skill sets is a rare and powerful trait. It's what allowed me to excel in tennis while simultaneously discovering talents I never knew I had, like poetry and art. It's what helped me navigate conflict, adapt to challenges, and ultimately find my path in life.

This book is not just a guide—it's a promise. If the void is in our blood, then it is also in our power to shape it. Together, we can turn what once felt like a curse into a legacy of resilience and mastery. If you ever find yourself standing at the edge of the void, know this: you are not alone, and you are more than capable of conquering it. This is our legacy, and it is one of strength, understanding, and infinite potential.

Navigating the Void

Chapter 4: The Struggles of Multiplicity

The Struggles of Multiplicity

"Who am I when I am not me? And who am I when I am too many?"

The human mind, as intricate as it is resilient, isn't designed to function as a chorus of voices vying for control. Living with multiple personas is not simply about sharing mental space; it is a complex and often exhausting dance between order and chaos. Each persona serves a purpose, yet their coexistence creates struggles that ripple through every aspect of life—internal battles, relationships, self-perception, and even mundane daily routines. These struggles, while deeply personal, are amplified by societal norms that demand simplicity in identity and uniformity in behavior.

The Fractured Mirror: Confusion Over Identity

One of the most profound struggles of living with multiple personas is grappling with a fractured sense of self. For most people, identity feels like a cohesive narrative—a singular "I" that weaves together their experiences, choices, and memories into a continuous story. It's something they rarely question, a steady thread that ties their past, present, and future into a recognizable whole.

For someone living with multiplicity, that singularity becomes a fleeting, almost mythical concept. Instead of a single thread, it feels like a thousand strands pulling in different directions, each persona weaving its own version of reality. What emerges is not a single narrative but a kaleidoscope of shifting identities, each stepping forward to interpret the world through its own unique lens.

I remember one evening, standing in front of the bathroom mirror, staring into my reflection, and feeling like I didn't know the person looking back at me. On some days, I could recognize the steady, confident gaze of **Nikolai (Pride)**— the persona who took pride in keeping things in order, the one who held my life together when it felt like it might shatter.

But there were other days—days when the reflection felt like someone else entirely. On one such day, I saw **Silas (Wrath)** staring back at me, his fiery anger simmering just below the surface. His eyes carried a heat that wasn't mine, a fierce intensity that seemed ready to lash out at the world. Other times, the gaze in the mirror softened, and I knew it was **Ravenna (Lust)** who had taken over, her longing for connection and creativity almost palpable. Her vulnerability seeped into my own eyes, making me feel exposed, almost raw.

It wasn't just the eyes—it was the way my body felt, the way my thoughts shifted as each persona stepped forward. Silas's presence came with a tightening in my chest, a surge of energy that felt impossible to contain. Ravenna, by contrast, brought a yearning sadness, a pull toward self-expression that I couldn't always articulate. Nikolai carried an almost oppressive weight of responsibility, his thoughts sharp and structured, his voice commanding me to maintain control.

Each time a persona emerged, it carried with it its own emotional palette, its own perspective, and its own definition of who "I" was. But with each shift, the question grew louder: *Who am I, really?*

Identity Lost in the Gaps

This confusion wasn't confined to quiet moments of introspection. It seeped into my daily life, disrupting the very fabric of my existence.

I'll never forget the science fair at school. My teacher pulled me aside afterward, her face glowing with pride as she congratulated me on my sharp, articulate presentation. She said I'd captivated the judges, answering their questions with a clarity that left them in awe. I should have felt proud—except I didn't remember being there.

It was as if someone had borrowed my body, stepped onto the stage, and lived an entire moment of my life without me. The memories were gone, swallowed by the Void.

Later, during tennis practice, I found myself at the center of another strange interaction. A teammate mentioned how quiet I had been that day and how unusual it was for me to stay so withdrawn during drills. I couldn't explain it, not to him or to myself. I didn't even remember walking onto the court.

These gaps in my memory weren't just disorienting—they were terrifying. They left me questioning not just my actions but my very existence.

If I can't remember being there, does it mean I wasn't?

If I wasn't "me" in those moments, then who was?

Each blank space felt like a piece of my identity had been stolen, leaving me to wonder if I was anything more than a collection of fragmented selves.

The Isolation of Being Many

The world around me didn't have the answers I sought. My teachers, my peers, even my family—they saw me as one person, a single individual with a single identity. They praised my achievements, remarked on my moods, and commented on my behavior, all without realizing that the "me" they were speaking to might not be the same "me" they had interacted with the day before.

It was isolating, this constant dissonance between how others perceived me and how I perceived myself. My friends spoke of shared experiences that I couldn't recall, moments I couldn't claim as my own. My family made assumptions about who I was based on glimpses of Nikolai's discipline, Silas's outbursts, or Ravenna's creativity, never realizing how incomplete their understanding truly was.

On the outside, I seemed whole. But inside, I felt like a fractured mirror, each shard reflecting a different version of myself. The reflection was never steady, never singular.

And the more I tried to hold onto one identity, the more it seemed to slip through my fingers.

Living with multiplicity means living in a state of constant flux, where identity is not a fixed point but a shifting mosaic of selves. It is a struggle to find balance, to reconcile the many voices within, and to answer the question that lingers at the heart of it all: *Who am I when I am too many?*

The Blackouts: Struggles with Memory Gaps and Dissociation

Perhaps the most terrifying aspect of living with multiple personas is the blackouts—those silent stretches of time where my consciousness is stolen, leaving only the aftermath to remind me that something, or someone, else was in control. It's not just the loss of memory that's unsettling; it's the dissociation itself. What begins as a defense mechanism—a way for the mind to shield itself from overwhelming stress—feels like a betrayal when it goes too far.

One moment, I could be walking home from school, thoughts wandering aimlessly as I rehearsed lines for a science presentation. The next, I'd find myself sitting on a park bench miles away, my feet aching as though I'd walked for hours. How had I gotten there? Why was I there? The questions screamed in my mind, but the answers were buried in the Void.

The Night Under the Streetlamps

One of the most harrowing blackouts I experienced came late one night.

I woke up shivering, the icy bite of the night air clawing at my skin. The world around me was bathed in the cold, artificial glow of street lamps, their flickering light casting long shadows on the pavement. My body ached in ways I couldn't explain—my legs trembled as though I'd been running for miles, and my hands were scraped and bruised, the dried blood on my knuckles catching the faint light.

I stood slowly, my heart pounding as I turned to take in my surroundings. I didn't recognize the street, the houses, or the neighborhood. Panic surged through me, sharp and suffocating.

Had I been in danger? Had someone hurt me? Or worse... had I hurt someone else?

The fear of not knowing was almost unbearable. My mind raced, piecing together fragments that didn't exist, desperately trying to reconstruct a memory that wasn't mine.

Eventually, I stumbled my way home, each step heavy with unease. When I finally crawled into bed, I didn't sleep. I lay there, staring at the ceiling as the weight of the unknown pressed down on me. My chest ached with the questions I couldn't answer, my thoughts spiraling into the Void where the memory of that night should have been.

The Quiet Blackouts

Not all blackouts came with bruises and terror. Some were quieter, more insidious, leaving behind fragments of lives I didn't remember living.

There was the notebook, its pages filled with Ravenna's sketches of strangers whose faces I didn't recognize. Her lines were raw and haunting, capturing emotions I hadn't consciously felt—longing, sorrow, passion. Her poetry was the same, scrawled across the margins in jagged handwriting that was undeniably mine but carried a voice that wasn't.

Then there was the spreadsheet. Meticulously organized, its rows and columns detailed personal finances I hadn't thought to track. The precision of it, the logic, the unmistakable ambition—it was Isidore's work, not mine. His focus was absolute, and his hunger for control was evident in every formula. I stared at the screen for what felt like hours, marveling at the complexity while feeling utterly unmoored.

These blackouts weren't as physically jarring as waking up in an unfamiliar neighborhood, but they were no less unsettling. Each fragment of a life lived without me reminded me that my mind was a house with too many rooms. Each door was locked, but I could hear the faint echo of voices behind them, whispering stories I wasn't meant to hear.

The Fight That Wasn't Mine

The most disturbing blackout happened at school during a confrontation with bullies.

It started like many such encounters had before. A group of boys—four or five, though I can't remember exactly—cornered me in the hallway. Their laughter echoed off the lockers, sharp and cruel. I don't recall everything they said, but the sting of humiliation is a feeling I'll never forget. My cheeks burned, my chest tightened, and the helplessness clawed at my throat like a caged animal.

And then—nothing.

The next thing I knew, I was sitting in the principal's office. My knuckles were raw, swollen, and caked with dried blood. My chest heaved with the remnants of adrenaline, and the room swam around me in a blur of harsh lighting and accusatory glares.

Across the room, two of the boys were being tended to by the school nurse. One had a broken nose, blood still streaming down his face, while the other cradled his arm, the swelling suggesting a break. The rest were gone, whisked away to the hospital, I was told.

The principal's voice was a distant hum, her words blending into the background as she berated me for my "violent outburst." She demanded an explanation, her tone sharp with anger and disbelief.

But I had nothing to say.

I didn't remember throwing a punch. I didn't remember swinging my fists or hearing their cries. All I remembered was the heat of their taunts, the helpless rage that had risen in my chest—and then the blankness.

Silas had taken over.

It was his rage, not mine, that had surged forward. His fists, not mine, had struck out in a fury. His wrath had consumed the moment, leaving me to deal with the consequences.

Living in the Aftermath

These blackouts left me feeling like a stranger in my own life. They weren't just gaps in memory—they were a loss of control, a surrendering of myself to the personas that lived within me. Each time, I was left to piece together the aftermath, to face the consequences of actions I couldn't remember taking.

There were moments when I feared the Void would swallow me completely, that the person I thought I was would vanish entirely, leaving only the fragments behind. But even in the chaos, a part of me clung to the hope that I could learn to navigate this strange, fractured existence.

Because of all the fear and confusion, there was something undeniable about the personas who stepped forward in my absence: they weren't just random intrusions. They were purposeful, even if their methods were extreme. Silas had protected me from the bullies when I couldn't protect myself. Ravenna had given voice to emotions I couldn't face. Isidore had created order where I saw only chaos.

They weren't enemies. They were parts of me, even if I didn't yet know how to live with them.

The blackouts were terrifying, but they were also a reminder that the Void wasn't empty. It was alive, teeming with voices and stories I had yet to understand. And though

I feared the darkness, I began to realize that in its depths lay the key to understanding myself.

The Loneliness of Multiplicity: Impact on Relationships

Living with multiple personas inevitably takes a toll on relationships. Trust, the cornerstone of any connection, becomes fragile when you don't fully understand your own actions. How could I expect others to believe in me when I often couldn't believe in myself? How could they rely on me when I didn't always know which version of myself they'd encounter?

It's not just the unpredictability of my interactions that complicates things—it's the way my personas pull me in different directions, each with its own social dynamics, needs, and struggles. Friendships, romantic relationships, even fleeting acquaintances—all are colored by the personas that emerge, creating a web of confusion and inconsistency that often leaves me feeling isolated, even among people who care about me.

Friendships Across Personas

Friendships were particularly challenging. On the surface, they should have been a source of comfort and stability, a refuge from the chaos within. But the reality was far more complicated. Each persona brought its own approach to social dynamics, shaping how I interacted with those around me.

Take **Nikolai**, for example. As the natural leader, he excelled in social situations, navigating conversations with ease and projecting a calm, steady demeanor that others found reassuring. He thrived in environments where control and confidence were key, and many people gravitated toward him. But Nikolai's perfectionism often made relationships feel transactional—more about maintaining order and meeting expectations than forming genuine connections.

Then there was **Silas**, whose intensity often scared people away. His presence was commanding, almost overwhelming, and while it could inspire respect, it just as often bred discomfort. Silas didn't do small talk; he thrived in confrontation, in pushing boundaries, in speaking truths others might prefer to avoid. His honesty, while refreshing to some, was too raw for many.

And then there was **Ravenna**, who craved meaningful, emotional connections but struggled with the vulnerability they required. She would open herself up to people, only to pull back when the depth of her feelings became too overwhelming. This push-and-pull dynamic created inconsistencies in my friendships that confused and alienated my peers, leaving many unsure of where they stood with me—or who I even was.

The Cracks in Friendship

One friendship stands out—a bond that had once been unshakable but which ultimately fractured under the weight of my multiplicity. Ethan and I had been inseparable since childhood, sharing secrets, dreams, and a thousand small moments that had formed the foundation of our connection. He was the kind of friend who felt like family, someone I believed would always be there.

But as my personas grew more active, the cracks in our friendship began to show. Ethan started noticing the inconsistencies before I fully understood them myself. He would point out how my tone changed mid-conversation, how I sometimes seemed distant or distracted, or how my responses didn't align with things I'd said just days before.

The breaking point came one afternoon, during a quiet moment after class. Ethan confronted me, his voice tinged with frustration and hurt.

"Why have you been so distant?" he asked, his eyes searching mine for an answer I didn't know how to give. "It's like you're not even the same person anymore."

He recounted conversations I couldn't remember, moments where I had ignored him or acted completely out of character. He mentioned times when I had been unusually cold, brushing off his attempts to talk, and others when I'd seemed overly emotional, confiding in him about things he didn't think I'd ever care to share.

I wanted to explain, but how do you tell someone that your mind doesn't always belong to you? How do you admit that the person they're speaking to might not be the one who spoke to them yesterday? The words stuck in my throat, and all I could offer was an apology that felt as hollow as the gaps in my memory.

Ethan tried to understand, but over time, the strain of my inconsistencies wore him down. Our conversations grew shorter, our interactions less frequent. Eventually, the bond that had once felt unbreakable faded into a quiet, mutual distance.

The Pain of Romantic Relationships

If friendships were challenging, romantic relationships were almost impossible. They demanded a level of consistency and intimacy that my multiplicity made difficult to maintain.

My first girlfriend, Sarah, was patient and kind in ways I didn't think I deserved. She saw something in me that I couldn't see in myself, and for a time, I believed that her steady presence might anchor me in the chaos.

But even Sarah couldn't navigate the complexities of my mind. She would often comment on how "different" I seemed from day to day, her voice tinged with a mixture of curiosity and concern. She'd laugh about how dating me felt like dating multiple people at once, unaware of how deeply her words cut.

One day, after a particularly confusing argument, she looked at me with an expression I couldn't quite read.

"Sometimes I don't know who I'm talking to," she said. "It's like… you're here, but you're not really *you*."

Her words lingered in the air, heavy and unanswerable. I wanted to tell her the truth, to explain the personas that shaped me, but the fear of being misunderstood—of being seen as broken—held me back. Instead, I deflected, assuring her that everything was fine, even as the distance between us grew.

Over time, the strain became too much. Sarah tried to bridge the gaps, but the inconsistencies in my behavior left her feeling as though she was reaching for a moving target. Eventually, we drifted apart, leaving me with an even deeper sense of isolation.

The Weight of Loneliness

The loneliness of multiplicity isn't just about the difficulty of forming connections—it's about the feeling of being fundamentally misunderstood. It's about the dissonance between how others perceive you and how you perceive yourself and the fear that even those who care for you will never truly understand the shifting mosaic of your identity.

Every relationship becomes a balancing act, a constant negotiation between the personas that shape your interactions. And even when those relationships are strong, the weight of your own inconsistencies can make them feel fragile.

Living with multiplicity is not just a challenge of the self—it is a challenge of connection. It is the struggle to let others in when you aren't always sure who they're meeting and the fear that even the strongest bonds might fracture under the weight of your many selves.

And yet, for all its challenges, multiplicity teaches you the value of those connections, however fleeting they may be.

It reminds you that even in the face of isolation, the desire to be understood is a thread that ties us all together.

The Battle for Self-Esteem

The most insidious consequence of living with these personas is the quiet war they wage on self-esteem. How do you feel confident in yourself when the idea of "self" feels as fragile and fleeting as smoke? It's not the loud battles that wear you down—it's the subtle erosion, the constant shifting of identity, and the lingering questions about who you really are.

I can't count the number of days I felt like a fraud, standing on a stage I hadn't auditioned for, performing lines someone else had written. Victories that should have brought pride felt hollow. Winning a tennis match wasn't satisfying when I knew it was **Elior (Envy)** driving me, his relentless voice goading me into perfection. Writing a beautiful poem felt like cheating when the words spilled onto the page like a river, whispered by **Ravenna (Lust)**, her creative fire burning too brightly to be mine alone.

Even my failures didn't feel like my own. When mistakes happened, I never knew whose fault they were. Was it **Silas (Wrath)**, letting anger cloud my judgment? Was **Noah (Sloth)** too passive to intervene? Or was it simply me, the conductor, who couldn't keep the orchestra in tune? The uncertainty gnawed at me, hollowing out my belief in myself piece by piece.

And then there were the memory gaps. Those were the worst. A missed conversation, a forgotten appointment, or a look of disappointment in someone's eyes when they realized I didn't remember what I'd promised. Each one felt like an indictment, evidence of a deeper fracture.

My mother noticed before I did. She was always practical and grounded, the kind of woman who believed every problem had a solution if you were willing to work for it. When my dissociation became impossible to ignore, she took me to therapy.

The therapist—calm, clinical, with a voice like the ticking of a metronome—listened to my fragmented explanations with the patience of someone used to broken stories. She suggested journaling, a way to "connect with my personas," as though they were pen pals I could write to.

I started reluctantly, my first entry little more than a shaky scrawl on a blank page. But then the words came—rushed, frantic, desperate. Each persona seemed eager to speak, their voices flooding the pages as though they'd been waiting for permission. At first, it was overwhelming. Reading back through the entries was like holding letters from strangers, their thoughts and feelings starkly different from my own.

"Do you know who I am?" one entry read, written in **Ravenna's** looping, elegant hand. "Do you know what I've given you?"

Another was scrawled with jagged strokes, **Silas's** unmistakable tone burning through the ink: "You're weak. You let them take over. You never fight."

And yet another, cool and precise, undoubtedly **Isidore (Greed)**: "If you want control, you need to plan. Without strategy, you'll always lose."

It was as if they were alive, each one jostling for dominance, each one demanding to be heard. The journals became a battlefield, their entries clashing in tone and purpose.

Some nights, I would sit at my desk and stare at the pages, wondering if I would ever truly own my successes—or even my failures. Was I just the sum of their voices, the conductor of an orchestra I couldn't quiet? Or was there something more to me, a core beneath the layers, waiting to be uncovered?

I wish I could say that journaling solved everything, but it didn't. What it did do was force me to confront the fractures, to acknowledge the personas not as enemies but as parts of a whole. It was the first step, and like every first step, it was terrifying. But in the moments of terror, I found something I hadn't felt in years: a flicker of hope that one day, I might understand who I really was.

A Glimmer of Hope

Amid the storm of shifting voices and fractured moments, there were rare, fleeting glimmers of clarity. They didn't come often, but when they did, they felt like finding a lighthouse in an endless sea of fog. Those moments reminded me that I wasn't entirely alone in my chaos.

Journaling became more than an exercise; it was a lifeline. Through it, I began to communicate with my personas, not just as fragmented echoes of myself but as distinct entities with their own voices and their own wisdom to share. As I filled the pages, a surprising pattern emerged: each of them had something to offer, even if their contributions were often tangled in conflict.

Nikolai (Pride), unsurprisingly, was the first to step forward with a solution. "If this is to work," he wrote in his strong, deliberate hand, "we need order. Chaos cannot lead to chaos. I will take the helm."

His words were commanding, self-assured, but not unkind. Nikolai didn't see himself as superior to the others, merely necessary. He was the conductor, the mediator, the one who could weave their disparate voices into something resembling harmony. His suggestion was straightforward but bold: a system of "rules" to maintain balance.

Under his plan, Nikolai would remain the **primary persona**, ensuring continuity and minimizing the disorienting memory gaps that plagued me. The others—**Ravenna**, **Silas**, **Elior**, and the rest—would only take control when absolutely necessary and only when their particular strengths were required. Decisions would be collective, but leadership would rest firmly in his hands.

The idea wasn't perfect—it felt fragile, like trying to build a bridge over a chasm with mismatched planks—but it was a start.

I could feel the pushback almost immediately.

"Rules?!" scrawled **Silas (Wrath)**, his handwriting jagged and heavy. "Life doesn't follow the rules, Nikolai. You don't control me."

Ravenna (Lust) responded with elegant disdain: "Rules are chains. Creativity dies in chains. Surely you see that?"

And yet, beneath the resistance, there was a grudging respect for Nikolai's plan. Even **Isidore (Greed)**, with his ever-pragmatic tone, added a terse, "It's inefficient to function without a leader. I'll follow—for now."

What struck me most wasn't just their voices but the realization that they were engaging with one another through me. The pages of my journal became a meeting ground, a place where their conflicting desires and perspectives could coexist, even if only for a moment. For the first time, I wasn't just at the battleground. I was the mediator, the one who could bring them together.

The days that followed weren't easy. Nikolai's system worked—sometimes. Memory gaps became less frequent, though they didn't disappear entirely. There were still moments of rebellion when **Silas's** anger would surge, or **Elior's** competitiveness would override Nikolai's control. But in those moments, I felt a new kind of clarity: I could see the struggle as it happened, like watching a play unfold on a stage.

It was exhausting, but it was progress.

And in those rare moments of peace, I felt something I hadn't in years: a faint but undeniable sense of hope. Perhaps I wasn't broken. Perhaps the chaos didn't have to consume me.

Perhaps, just perhaps, I could find a way to become whole.

Closing Thought

To my son: If you ever find yourself walking this path, know that the struggles are real but not insurmountable. The challenges of multiplicity can feel overwhelming, but with time and effort, you can find balance. This chapter is not just a recounting of my hardships—it is a reminder that even in the darkest moments, there is always a way forward. Hold onto that hope, and let it guide you.

Chapter 5: The Turning Point

The Turning Point

"Sometimes, the darkest moments are the clearest mirrors, reflecting not just who you are, but who you have the potential to become."

Rock bottom is not a place; it is a moment. It is the weight of everything you've avoided crashing down at once, forcing you to face truths you've hidden from even yourself. For me, it wasn't a single moment but a series of events that shattered the fragile illusion of control I thought I had over my life. The personas that had once acted as shields were now running wild, creating chaos I could no longer ignore. It was in this chaos that I found clarity—a realization that these fragments of myself were not curses but keys to understanding and, ultimately, harmony.

The Fight That Changed Everything

The first of these moments came during a high school basketball game. By then, **Silas (Wrath)** had already made his presence known in my life. His rage and determination had been both a blessing and a curse, pushing me to excel in physical activities while also making me volatile in moments of stress.

On this particular day, we were up against a rival school, and the tension was palpable. The game was close, the air thick with adrenaline, and the crowd's cheers blurred into a deafening roar. One bad call from the referee sent my temper spiraling. I felt a switch flip inside me—the unmistakable pull of **Silas** taking control.

What happened next is a haze in my memory, a series of disconnected images and sounds. I remember shoving an opponent so hard that he crashed into the bleachers. I remember the coach shouting my name, his voice filled with anger and disbelief. And then, nothing.

I came back to myself in the locker room, surrounded by my teammates, their faces a mixture of fear and confusion. "What the hell was that, man?" one of them asked. I couldn't answer. I didn't even know what "that" was.

The fallout was swift and severe. I was benched for the rest of the season, my coach citing "uncontrollable behavior" as the reason. My father, furious, grounded me indefinitely, calling me a disgrace to the family. But the worst part wasn't the punishment—it was the growing realization that I was losing control of my life.

The Night in the Park

The second turning point came months later, on a cold autumn night. I woke up on a park bench, disoriented and freezing, with no memory of how I had gotten there. The park was nearly an hour's walk from my house, and the last thing I remembered was falling asleep in my bed.

Panic gripped me as I tried to piece together what had happened. My clothes were dirty, my shoes scuffed, and there was a faint taste of blood in my mouth. Had I been in a fight? Had **Silas** taken over again? I had no answers, only questions that filled me with dread.

Walking home in the dark, I couldn't shake the feeling that I was unsafe—not because of the world around me, but because of myself. I didn't trust my own mind, my own body. Who was I when I wasn't me? And how could I protect myself from something that lived inside me?

The Therapy Session

Desperate for answers, my mother arranged for me to see a therapist. She was a no-nonsense woman with sharp eyes and a calm demeanor, the kind of person who could see through any facade. After listening to my fragmented stories of memory gaps, uncontrollable episodes, and inexplicable actions, she introduced me to the concept of dissociation.

"This isn't something you can medicate away," she said, her voice steady but compassionate. "But it's not something you have to face alone. We can work on understanding these parts of you, finding a way to bring them into harmony."

Her suggestion was simple but revolutionary: journaling. By keeping a record of my thoughts, feelings, and actions, I could start to identify patterns and, perhaps, communicate with the parts of myself that seemed to exist beyond my awareness.

At first, I was skeptical. How could writing in a notebook solve a problem that felt so overwhelming? But with no other options, I decided to give it a try.

Conversations with the Void

The first few weeks of journaling were uneventful. I wrote about my day-to-day life, my frustrations, and my fears. But then, something strange happened. One morning, I opened my notebook to find entries I didn't remember writing.

The handwriting was mine, but the tone and content were foreign. **Silas** had written about his anger—how he felt like I only called on him when I needed to fight but ignored him the rest of the time. **Ravenna (Lust)** wrote a poem about feeling unseen, her words dripping with longing. **Nikolai (Pride)**, ever the leader, had left me a list of suggestions for maintaining control.

At first, it was unnerving. But as the days turned into weeks, I began to see the potential in these exchanges. My personas weren't just fragments—they were voices, each with their own needs, strengths, and perspectives.

Through journaling, I learned to listen. **Silas**, for all his rage, was deeply protective, his anger stemming from a desire to keep me safe. **Ravenna's** creativity wasn't just about expression—it was her way of connecting to the world. **Nikolai's** lists, while sometimes overwhelming, were his attempt to bring order to the chaos.

The Realization

The turning point wasn't a single moment of epiphany but a gradual shift in perspective. I began to see my personas not as enemies to be controlled but as allies to be understood.

Each one brought something valuable to the table, and when they worked together, I felt whole in a way I never had before.

The key, I realized, was balance. **Nikolai's** leadership was crucial, but it couldn't come at the expense of the others. **Silas** needed outlets for his energy that didn't involve violence. **Ravenna** needed time and space to create without fear of judgment. By acknowledging and honoring these needs, I could begin to harmonize the chaos within me.

Closing Thought

To my son: If you ever find yourself at rock bottom, know that it is not the end. It is a crossroads, a place where you can choose to rebuild yourself stronger than before. The struggles of multiplicity are real and daunting, but they are not insurmountable.

This chapter is a testament to the power of self-awareness and the importance of seeking help when you need it. You do not have to face the Void alone. Embrace the turning points, no matter how painful they may seem, for they are the moments that will define your journey.

Let this be your guide, your map through the darkness. And remember: even in the chaos, there is always a path forward. You just have to find it.

Chapter 6: Building Harmony Among Shadows

Building Harmony Among Shadows

"The key to surviving the shadows within is not to silence them, but to guide them, weaving their voices into a symphony rather than letting them erupt into a cacophony."

Living with multiple personas is akin to standing at the helm of a ship with a mutinous crew—each one with their own idea of the best course to steer. The challenge isn't in silencing these voices but in understanding their purpose, learning to listen to them, and guiding them in unison. It's not an easy journey; it requires patience, self-awareness, and constant effort. But when balance is achieved, the rewards are immense—a life not defined by chaos but enhanced by the unique strengths of each voice within.

Recognizing Who's in Control

Identifying which persona is in control is the first step in building harmony. Their influence often reveals itself in subtle ways—a shift in posture, a change in tone, or even the way I think. At other times, their presence is impossible to ignore, a tidal wave of emotion or action that takes over completely.

When **Silas (Wrath)** takes the light, for instance, my senses sharpen, and my body feels like it's bracing for battle. He's pure adrenaline, a force of nature that takes control in moments of conflict or perceived danger. I remember one evening when I was walking home and noticed someone following me. My heart began to race, but it wasn't fear—it was readiness. **Silas** had stepped forward, his instincts taking over. By the time I reached my door, the follower had long since vanished, unnerved by the silent confidence radiating from me. Only later did I realize how effortlessly **Silas** had taken control, keeping me safe without panic or hesitation.

Ravenna (Lust) brings a different kind of influence. When she emerges, the world slows, and my perspective shifts to one of raw emotion and beauty. I'll find myself drawn to the flicker of candlelight or the sound of distant music, her creativity whispering through every action. During one such moment, I spent hours sketching a single rose, captivated by its delicate folds and shadows. When the drawing was finished, it wasn't just a rose—it was a story, a piece of art that spoke to something deeper than words could convey.

Each persona leaves traces of their presence, and over time, I've learned to recognize these signs. A clenched jaw signals **Silas**, while meticulous organization is **Nikolai's (Pride)** hallmark. When I find myself questioning my abilities or striving to outdo someone, it's **Elior (Envy)** nudging me forward. These clues are my map, guiding me toward a better understanding of the internal dynamics at play.

Listening to Each Voice

Every persona has a voice, and learning to listen to them is like turning into a complex radio frequency. Their perspectives are unique, shaped by their roles and the emotions they embody. Ignoring them only leads to discord; understanding them opens the door to harmony.

Silas (Wrath): His voice is the loudest, often coming as a roar of defiance or a growl of warning. He doesn't mince words, and his demands are simple: protect, survive, conquer. While his methods are sometimes extreme, I've come to realize that **Silas's** intentions are always rooted in a desire to shield me from harm.

*In high school, I once found myself cornered by an aggressive teammate after a tennis match. His accusations were baseless, but his tone was threatening. **Silas** surged forward, his voice commanding and unyielding. I didn't lash out physically, but my response was so firm, so full of power, that the teammate backed down immediately.*

Ravenna (Lust): Her voice is soft, almost musical, and often comes in the form of imagery or poetic phrases. She craves connection, beauty, and expression, and her influence is a balm in moments of emotional chaos.

*After a particularly rough day, I found myself wandering through a park at sunset. The sky was a blaze of orange and pink, and **Ravenna** whispered, "Capture this." I pulled out a sketchpad I hadn't used in months and began drawing. By the time the sun had set, I felt a calm I hadn't experienced in weeks.*

Elior (Envy): **Elior's** voice is sharp, questioning, and often challenging. He pushes me to be better and to strive for more, but his words can cut deep if left unchecked.

*During a college group project, I found myself comparing my contributions to others. "Is this enough?" **Elior** asked, his tone laced with dissatisfaction. At first, his critique stung, but it also drove me to refine my work, turning in a presentation that earned praise from both my professor and peers.*

Listening to these voices doesn't mean surrendering to them. It means understanding their motivations and integrating their perspectives into a broader framework of decision-making.

The Role of the Lead Persona

Nikolai (Pride) is the steady hand on the wheel, the one who keeps the ship from capsizing. As the lead persona, he has a unique ability to mediate between the others, ensuring their voices are heard without allowing any single one to dominate. When **Nikolai** is in control, there's a sense of calm and order—a balance that feels almost effortless.

But **Nikolai's** role isn't just about maintaining control; it's about fostering collaboration. He listens to **Silas's** instincts, **Ravenna's** creativity, **Elior's** ambition, and **Noah's (Sloth)** quiet wisdom, weaving their input into a cohesive strategy. In many ways, **Nikolai** acts as a translator, helping me understand the language of my personas and guiding their energy toward constructive outcomes.

*During a particularly hectic week at work, I found myself juggling multiple deadlines, each demanding a different set of skills. **Nikolai** stepped forward, organizing the chaos with precision. He allowed **Silas** to channel his intensity* *into completing tasks under pressure, **Ravenna** to infuse creativity into a presentation, and **Elior** to push me to refine my ideas. By the end of the week, I hadn't just survived—I had excelled, thanks to their collective effort under **Nikolai's** guidance.*

Practical Strategies for Harmony

Maintaining harmony among my personas is a daily practice, requiring intentional effort and self-awareness. These strategies have been instrumental in managing the complexity of the Void:

Morning Check-Ins: Each day begins with reflection, identifying which personas are most active and what they need. If **Silas** is restless, I plan physical activities to release his energy. If **Ravenna** feels stifled, I set aside time for creativity.

Journaling as Dialogue: My journal is a space for each persona to express themselves. By recording their thoughts and feelings, I've developed a better understanding of their motivations and how to address them.

Mindfulness and Grounding: Practices like meditation help me stay centered, allowing **Nikolai** to maintain control even when emotions run high.

External Accountability: Trusted friends and mentors act as sounding boards, helping me recognize when a person's influence is clouding my judgment.

To my son: The shadows within you are not obstacles—they are allies, waiting to be understood. Each persona is a part of you, a thread in the intricate tapestry of your identity. Their voices may sometimes clash, but they also have the potential to harmonize into something extraordinary.

This chapter is your guide to balance, a roadmap for navigating the complexities of multiplicity with grace and strength. Remember, you are not defined by any single persona. You are the symphony, the conductor, the master of your own mind. Use these tools to build harmony, and let the shadows within become your greatest source of power.

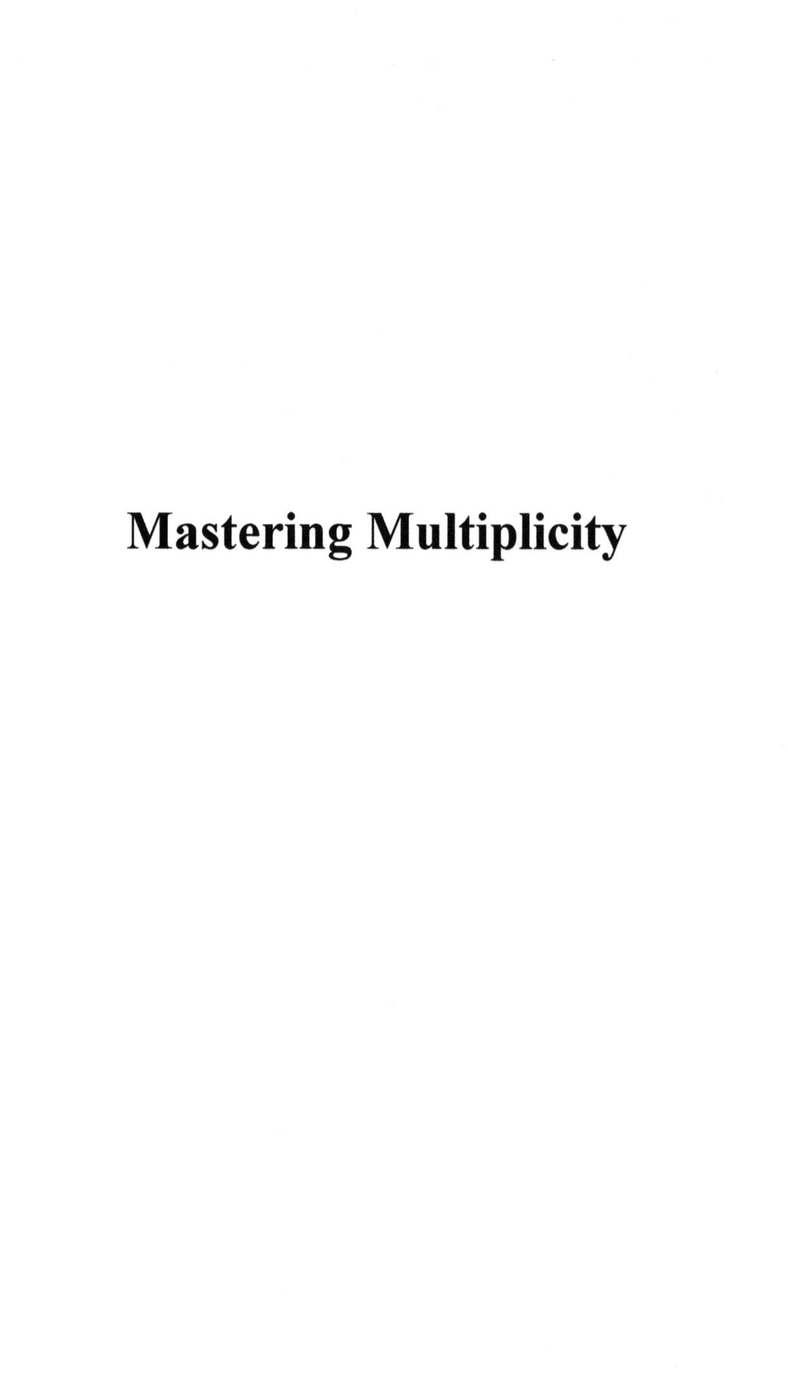

Mastering Multiplicity

Chapter 7: Embracing Strengths, Mitigating Weaknesses

Embracing Strengths, Mitigating Weaknesses

"Our greatest strengths often come from the same place as our deepest struggles. The key is not to deny either, but to learn how to wield one while tempering the other."

The personas within me are paradoxes. Each one is a gift wrapped in a curse, a strength bound tightly to its own weakness. They've shaped me, challenged me, and even saved me. But their power comes at a cost. I've had to learn to embrace what they offer without letting their excesses consume me. It's not easy to wield a double-edged sword without cutting yourself, but it's a skill you have to master if you want to survive.

Understanding Dualities

Strength and weakness are not opposites—they are often two sides of the same coin. Creativity can be a spark of brilliance, but without control, it becomes chaos. Confidence can lead to leadership, but unchecked, it turns into arrogance. This chapter isn't about silencing the personas or banishing their flaws. It's about understanding their dualities, finding balance, and wielding their strengths wisely.

When I first began to recognize the personas, I saw only their extremes. **Silas (Wrath)** was raw anger, a destructive force I couldn't contain. **Ravenna (Lust)** was a wellspring of inspiration, but her desires often left me scattered and unfocused. **Noah (Sloth)** seemed like a soothing balm, but his stillness quickly became inertia.

What I didn't see then was their potential. Silas wasn't just anger—he was also resilience, a protector who refused to let me crumble under pressure. Ravenna's creativity could bring focus and beauty when guided with intention. Noah's quiet presence wasn't just stillness—it was a reflection, a gift that helped me process the chaos.

The moment I began to see them as more than their extremes was the moment I began to reclaim control.

The Challenge of Balance

The real work was in finding balance. Letting **Elior (Envy)** drive me toward improvement without letting him drown me in comparisons. Giving **Selene (Gluttony)** space to remind me of life's pleasures without letting her lull me into complacency. It was like walking a tightrope, always aware that too much or too little of any persona could send me crashing down.

This process wasn't just about identifying strengths and weaknesses—it was about learning to listen. Each persona had something to say, and often, they spoke in conflict. But buried within that conflict were truths I needed to hear.

I've spent countless hours asking myself hard questions. Where does **Isidore (Greed)** end and my ambition begin? How much of my strength belongs to **Nikolai (Pride)**, and how much comes from me? These aren't questions with easy answers. Sometimes, they don't have answers at all.

But the act of asking, of exploring the shadows, is where the growth happens.

Harnessing the Power Within

If I've learned anything, it's this: the personas are not here to destroy me. They are parts of me, reflections of my struggles and my strengths. The chaos they bring is not an enemy to be defeated but a force to be understood and shaped.

By recognizing their dualities, I've begun to wield their strengths while mitigating their weaknesses. It's not a perfect process—I still stumble, still falter—but it's progress. And in that progress, I've found something that eluded me for so long: a sense of hope.

This chapter isn't just about my journey. It's about yours. Because we all have our shadows, our double-edged swords. The key isn't to deny them but to learn how to wield them without letting them wield you.

Ravenna (Lust): The Muse of Creativity and Connection

"Art isn't just what I create—it's what I live. Every moment, every sensation, every fleeting spark of connection is a brushstroke on the canvas of existence."

Ravenna is the whisper of inspiration in the quiet hours, the sudden spark that turns an ordinary moment into something extraordinary. She lives for beauty, for passion, for the intangible forces that stir the soul. Her presence is magnetic, drawing others toward her with a warmth and vibrancy that feels almost otherworldly. But her brilliance comes with a shadow—her endless pursuit of connection and creativity can leave her untethered, chasing fleeting desires at the expense of what matters most.

Strengths: The Gifts of a Muse

Boundless Creativity:

Ravenna's gift is the ability to see the world in ways others cannot. A blank page is never empty in her hands; it is a universe waiting to be born. When she takes the light, ideas flow effortlessly, unrestrained by doubt or logic.

Late at night, when others sleep, Ravenna takes over. My hands, almost possessed, poured color onto the canvas. The strokes are wild and instinctive. When dawn breaks, a masterpiece I barely remember creating stares back at me—a haunting figure wrapped in gold and shadow, its eyes filled with unspoken sorrow.

Emotional Empathy:

Ravenna feels deeply, her ability to connect with others almost unsettling in its intensity. She doesn't just hear someone's story; she lives it, her heart beating in time with theirs.

In the middle of a tense conversation, I feel Ravenna's influence surge. The anger drains from my voice, replaced by an overwhelming need to understand. "Tell me," I find myself saying, "what's really hurting you?" The flood of emotion from the other person is as cathartic for me as it is for them.

Weaknesses: The Price of Passion

Distraction:

Ravenna's focus on beauty and connection can feel intoxicating, but it often comes at a cost. Deadlines slip by unnoticed. Promises are forgotten. Responsibilities are ignored in the pursuit of an elusive muse.

The cluttered desk is a testament to her influence. Sketches, notes, and fragments of poetry spill over, while unopened bills and unanswered emails sit untouched in the corner. I tell myself I'll deal with them later, but "later" feels like a foreign concept when Ravenna is in control.

Overindulgence:

Her pursuit of beauty sometimes crosses into obsession. A single project can consume me for days, or a fleeting moment of connection can leave me chasing someone who was never meant to stay.

The gallery was supposed to be a quick visit, but hours slipped by as I lost myself in the brushstrokes of a single painting. It's not enough to admire it; I need to feel what the artist felt and understand the exact moment their hand trembled on the canvas.

The Duality of Ravenna

Ravenna's brilliance is undeniable, but she must be tempered. When left unchecked, her passions burn too brightly, consuming everything in their path. Yet, without her, life would be colorless, devoid of the magic she brings.

One day, in the middle of an important meeting, I felt Ravenna stir. The words being spoken are dull lifeless, and my mind begins to wander. A phrase from the presenter becomes a spark, igniting an idea for a story I've been struggling to write. Before I realize it, I've tuned out completely, my fingers sketching madly in the margins of my notes.

When the meeting ends, the story is complete, but I have no memory of the agreements I was supposed to review. Ravenna's creation comes with a cost—and I'm left to deal with the fallout.

Strategies to Work With Ravenna

Creative Boundaries:

To honor Ravenna without losing control, I've learned to set clear boundaries. Creative time is sacred, but it has limits. She can take over during those hours, but outside of them, I remind her that structure isn't the enemy—it's the foundation for her freedom.

Balancing Connection and Solitude:

While Ravenna thrives on interaction, she also needs time alone. I schedule moments of quiet reflection, giving her space to draw from within instead of always seeking inspiration from others.

Ravenna's Role in the Narrative

Ravenna is the persona that transforms the mundane into the extraordinary. She is the spark in moments of despair, the light that turns pain into beauty. But she is also a warning—a reminder of the price of unchecked passion.

Her story within me is one of balance: to let her create without letting her consume, to embrace her gifts without losing myself in her desires.

Isidore (Greed): The Strategist and Planner

"In a world of uncertainty, preparation is power. To see beyond the moment and control what you can—that is how you survive."

Isidore is the architect of foresight, a master of strategy who thrives on preparation and accumulation. His presence sharpens every decision, ensuring that risks are mitigated and opportunities seized. But his focus on control and resources comes with a cost—when unchecked, and his meticulous nature can spiral into obsession, leaving little room for spontaneity or trust in others.

Strengths: The Power of Precision

Strategic Thinking:

Isidore's mind is a chessboard, always five steps ahead. He sees paths others miss, making him invaluable in moments of uncertainty. His ability to anticipate and adapt has saved me from countless missteps.

During a work crisis, deadlines loom, and panic spreads. Isidore steps in. His calm voice silences the chaos as he lays out a step-by-step plan, assigning tasks with unflinching precision. By the end of the day, the impossible is accomplished—not because of luck, but because of his relentless focus.

Resilience in Pursuit:

Isidore's determination knows no limits. He is the force that ensures goals are met, no matter the obstacles. When others might falter, he presses on, calculating the next move with unyielding resolve.

After hours of failed attempts at fixing a crucial piece of code, exhaustion pulls at me. But Isidore refuses to quit. "Focus," he says, his voice firm. Slowly, methodically, I retrace my steps, and when the solution finally clicks, it's his persistence that carries me through.

Weaknesses: The Cost of Control

Obsessive Behavior:

Isidore's need for control often becomes a double-edged sword. His meticulous planning can paralyze me, trapping me in endless analysis when action is needed.

A seemingly simple decision—choosing a flight for an upcoming trip—turns into a full-day endeavor. Tabs pile up on my screen as I compare prices, routes, and reviews, but I am unable to commit. By the time I make the choice, exhaustion has already set in, and I've missed the best option.

Emotional Detachment:

Isidore's focus on logic makes it difficult to connect with others emotionally. He views relationships as transactions, analyzing them for value rather than meaning.

A friend shares their struggles, their voice heavy with vulnerability. But instead of offering comfort, I hear Isidore's voice calculating solutions. "What you should do is..." I begin, only to see the disappointment in their eyes.

The Duality of Isidore

Isidore's strength lies in his clarity and discipline, but his obsession with perfection can make him rigid, leaving no room for the unpredictable beauty of life. His hunger for control is both his power and his burden.

An unexpected opportunity arises—an impromptu trip to meet a friend in need. Isidore resists, his voice cold and practical: "This wasn't in the plan. What about your deadlines? Your finances?" But something in me knows that this moment matters: that plans can be rewritten. As I pack my bag, I feel Isidore retreating, his disapproval palpable. The trip was chaotic and unstructured, but it was exactly what I needed.

Strategies to Work With Isidore

Set Clear Goals:

By defining specific objectives, I give Isidore a framework to channel his energy productively, preventing him from spiraling into unnecessary planning.

Balance Logic with Emotion:

I remind Isidore that not everything can be calculated. Sometimes, the best decisions come from the heart, not the mind.

Isidore's Role in the Narrative

Isidore is the strategist, the one who ensures I am never unprepared. He is my shield against chaos, my guide through complexity. But his strength lies in balance—letting him lead when needed while reminding him that life isn't just a series of calculated moves.

His story is one of trust: trusting in his plans without letting them define me and trusting that not every moment needs a strategy.

Silas (Wrath): The Protector and Warrior

"The shield and sword, unyielding in the face of threats, but quick to ignite."

Silas is the embodiment of strength, a guardian who rises in the face of danger and confrontation. He is my unwavering protector, the force that refuses to let me crumble under pressure. With Silas, I feel an unparalleled resilience, both physical and emotional, that allows me to face challenges with an almost primal determination. But his power is volatile—a fire that burns as easily as it shields. When unchecked, his rage can become destructive, turning allies into enemies and solutions into chaos.

Strengths: The Fire of Resilience

Physical Power:

Silas's influence brings an almost supernatural physicality. My body feels stronger, my reflexes sharper, and my endurance unbreakable. He thrives in moments where the action is required, channeling fear into raw energy.

The attacker lunged at me, a blur of movement and menace. Silas surged forward, taking control. My muscles tensed, my grip steady as I deflected the blow and countered with precision. The fight ended in seconds, my breath steady as though the fear had never existed.

Emotional Fortitude:

Silas isn't just physical strength—he is emotional armor. In moments of doubt or despair, his presence silences the inner chaos, replacing uncertainty with a fierce determination to push forward.

Standing before a crowd to deliver an unexpected speech, my hands trembled with nerves. Silas's voice cut through: "They're just people. Speak. Command." A calm, unshakable confidence settled over me, and each word I spoke felt deliberate and strong, as though nothing could throw me off balance.

Weaknesses: The Cost of Wrath

Uncontrolled Anger:

Silas's protective instincts can easily tip into aggression. His fire, meant to defend, lashes out, causing harm where none was intended.

An argument with a close friend spiraled as Silas took over. My voice rose, cutting through their defenses with unfiltered anger. The moment the silence hit, regret followed—it wasn't the battle I wanted to win.

Tunnel Vision:

Silas's singular focus on survival blinds him to nuance. In his world, it's fight or flight, and everything else fades into insignificance, often at the cost of long-term consequences.

A critical team meeting dissolved into a heated debate. Silas locked onto one dissenting voice, cutting them down

Strategies to Harness Silas

Channel Energy Constructively:

Silas thrives when given a purpose. Physical outlets like exercise, martial arts, or even manual labor provide him with a controlled way to release his intensity without collateral damage.

Pause Before Action:

When Silas begins to rise, I've learned to take a moment— a single deep breath, a count to five—to assess whether his reaction is warranted. This pause often softens his flames, redirecting them toward more measured actions.

Silas's Role in the Narrative

Silas is the warrior, the unyielding shield that protects me from fear and harm. He is a reminder of the power that comes from resilience and the strength found in standing firm. But his story is also a cautionary tale: strength without control can quickly turn into destruction.

To embrace Silas is to honor his fire while tempering it with wisdom, letting his protection guide me without letting his rage consume me.

Elior (Envy): The Relentless Competitor

"The challenger, pushing me to strive for greatness but sometimes clouded by comparison."

Elior is ambition personified, a driving force that refuses to settle for mediocrity. He is the spark that propels me forward, constantly measuring my progress against the successes of others. To Elior, every achievement is a challenge, every milestone a marker of what's possible. But his relentless pursuit of greatness comes with a shadow: the ever-present danger of comparison. When unchecked, Elior's voice turns from inspiration to doubt, making me feel inadequate even in the face of my accomplishments.

Strengths: The Fuel of Ambition

Ambition:

Elior's competitive nature drives me to exceed my limits. He sees obstacles as opportunities and refuses to accept anything less than excellence.

I was the underdog in a presentation competition, facing seasoned professionals. Elior whispered in my ear, "Why not you?" His voice pushed me to rehearse until my delivery was flawless. When the applause came, I realized that it wasn't just skill—it was Elior's relentless drive that had brought me to this moment.

Adaptability:

Elior thrives on challenges, forcing me to learn, grow, and adapt to new situations. His hunger to match or surpass others makes me fearless in exploring uncharted territory.

Watching a colleague excel at a skill I lacked, Elior's voice nudged me: "Learn it. Prove you can." Hours of late-night practice followed, and soon, I was presenting my own take on the skill, earning not just respect but a sense of pride in my adaptability.

Weaknesses: The Shadow of Comparison

Comparison Trap:

Elior's focus on others can make my own achievements feel hollow. Instead of celebrating victories, I find myself wondering if they measure up to someone else's.

Scrolling through social media, each success story felt like a jab. "They're doing better," Elior whispered. My thoughts spiraled, turning a productive day into a series of questions about why I wasn't achieving as much.

Impatience:

Elior's need for immediate results can overshadow the joy of the process. His voice grows restless when progress feels slow, pushing me to rush instead of savor.

While learning a new hobby, Elior grew frustrated at every mistake. "Why aren't you good at this yet?" he demanded. His impatience drained the joy from the experience, leaving me more focused on the end goal than the journey itself.

Strategies to Harness Elior

Set Personal Benchmarks:

Redirecting Elior's energy toward personal goals helps me focus on my own progress instead of others'. Measured against my own standards, his drive becomes a tool for growth rather than self-doubt.

Celebrate Achievements:

Acknowledging milestones, no matter how small, reminds Elior that the journey is as important as the destination. By celebrating progress, I temper his impatience and keep his ambition constructive.

Elior's Role in the Narrative

Elior is the persona who reminds me that growth comes from challenge. He is the voice that says, "You can do more," and the force that pushes me to rise. But his strength is tempered by the understanding that my path is mine alone. To work with Elior is to channel his ambition without letting the shadow of comparison cloud my sense of self.

Selene (Gluttony): The Comfort Seeker and Nurturer

"The one who indulges in life's pleasures, offering comfort but sometimes lacking restraint."

Selene is the warm embrace at the end of a long day, the voice that reminds me to pause and savor the small joys of life. She is the nurturer, always encouraging rest, relaxation, and self-care. With Selene in control, the chaos quiets, replaced by a soothing appreciation for the present moment. But her indulgence can become a trap. If left unchecked, Selene's pursuit of comfort tips into procrastination and excess, where the pleasures of life come at the expense of progress.

Strengths: The Gift of Comfort

Self-Care:

Selene ensures I prioritize my well-being. She pulls me back from the brink of burnout, reminding me that rest is not a luxury but a necessity.

After weeks of overworking, Selene's voice became impossible to ignore. "Stop. Breathe," she whispered as I stared blankly at my screen. Her influence guided me to prepare a hot bath, the scent of lavender filling the air. By the time I emerged, I felt renewed, and my body and mind were finally at peace.

Appreciation for Comfort:

Selene's presence helps me notice and cherish the beauty in everyday moments—a warm meal, a sunset, or the laughter of friends. She fosters gratitude and contentment, even in the simplest of experiences.

Sitting on the porch with a steaming cup of tea, Selene's voice was soft but clear: "Isn't this enough?" The golden light of the setting sun wrapped around me, and for the first time in weeks, I felt wholly present, savoring the stillness.

Weaknesses: The Cost of Indulgence

Overindulgence:

Selene's love for comfort can spiral into excess. Too much rest turns into stagnation, and small indulgences—like a treat or a break—become prolonged distractions.

Scene Example: What started as a plan for a short nap stretched into an entire afternoon in bed. Netflix autoplayed episode after episode, Selene's soothing voice encouraging me to stay wrapped in my blanket. By evening, the day had slipped away, the to-do list untouched.

Lack of Discipline:

Selene's focus on immediate gratification can overshadow the need for structure. Responsibilities take a backseat, and progress halts in the face of fleeting pleasures.

On a rare free weekend, I promised myself I'd catch up on projects. But Selene led me to the kitchen, and soon, I was lost in baking cookies I didn't need. The hours melted away in the scent of sugar and cinnamon, leaving tasks undone and a growing sense of guilt.

Strategies to Harness Selene

Balance Comfort with Discipline:

By setting boundaries, I allow Selene to nurture me without letting her influence disrupt progress. Scheduling specific times for rest ensures her presence remains restorative rather than excessive.

Incorporate Healthy Habits:

Guiding Selene toward activities that promote well-being—like cooking nutritious meals, enjoying nature, or practicing mindfulness—keeps her focus on positive comfort rather than indulgent distractions.

Selene's Role in the Narrative

Selene is the reminder that life is meant to be lived, not merely endured. She teaches the importance of finding joy and warmth in the present, ensuring I don't lose myself in the grind. But her story is also a lesson in moderation: comfort is vital, but only when balanced with purpose.

To work with Selene is to honor her gift of peace while tempering her excess, finding harmony between indulgence and intention.

Nikolai (Pride): The Leader and Mediator

"The one who guides the symphony, maintaining balance but burdened by the weight of control."

Nikolai is the anchor, the persona who holds everything together. He is the calm voice of reason amid chaos, the diplomat who ensures the personas coexist without tearing me apart. Nikolai's leadership brings order, clarity, and direction, allowing me to navigate challenges with confidence. Yet his strength is also his burden—his belief that everything rests on his shoulders can lead to isolation, overwork, and moments of quiet despair.

Strengths: The Gift of Leadership

Balance and Leadership:

Nikolai is the mediator, the one who aligns the personas into a cohesive whole. He ensures their conflicting desires are transformed into collective strengths, guiding me toward balanced decisions.

A major life decision loomed—whether to accept a new job offer or stay in my current role. Silas wanted the challenge, Ravenna craved the creative opportunities, and Isidore calculated the financial gains. Nikolai stepped forward, weighing their voices with care. "This isn't about one of us—it's about all of us," he said, his tone firm yet thoughtful. By the end, the choice felt clear—not because it was easy, but because it was aligned.

Self-Assurance:

Nikolai's unwavering confidence creates stability, even in moments of uncertainty. His composure allows me to face challenges with clarity, knowing that I can trust his judgment.

Standing before a panel of executives, the weight of the moment threatened to crack my resolve. But Nikolai's steady voice rang out: "You've done the work. Now show them." My shoulders straightened, my voice steady as I presented, each word carrying the strength of his assurance.

Weaknesses: The Burden of Control

Isolation:

Nikolai's deep sense of responsibility often isolates him. He hesitates to delegate, believing that only he can bear the weight of leadership.

A team project was spiraling out of control, but instead of asking for help, Nikolai took on every task himself. His insistence on managing everything left me exhausted, and though the project succeeded, the toll it took lingered for weeks.

Overburdened:

Nikolai's constant vigilance wears him down. His fear of failure keeps him on edge, making it difficult for him to rest or acknowledge his limits.

After days of juggling work, family, and personal obligations, Nikolai's voice became strained. "We can't stop," he insisted, even as my hands shook from exhaustion. His refusal to pause pushed me to the brink of burnout.

Strategies to Harness Nikolai

Delegate When Needed:

I remind Nikolai that leadership doesn't mean doing everything alone. By trusting other personas to take the light when appropriate, he lightens his load and allows their strengths to shine.

Practice Self-Compassion:

Encouraging Nikolai to recognize his limits and prioritize rest ensures that his leadership remains effective and sustainable. Small moments of self-care—like journaling or mindfulness—help him recharge.

Nikolai's Role in the Narrative

Nikolai is the conductor of the symphony, the leader who brings balance to chaos. He is the embodiment of rationality and composure, ensuring that no single persona dominates the whole. But his story is also a lesson in vulnerability: true leadership isn't about carrying every burden—it's about knowing when to let go.

To work with Nikolai is to honor his wisdom while reminding him that strength lies not just in control but in trust.

Noah (Sloth): The Stillness and Observer

"Sometimes, the greatest strength lies in doing nothing. In the quiet moments, where others rush, I pause, reflect, and find clarity."

Noah embodies stillness, a soothing presence that emerges when the chaos of life becomes overwhelming. He is the persona that pulls me back from the brink, reminding me that there is power in rest, observation, and contemplation. Noah doesn't push or pull—he simply waits, allowing the noise to subside until the path forward becomes clear. Yet, his stillness comes with a cost. If left unchecked, his quiet retreat can turn into avoidance, paralyzing me in moments when action is required.

Strengths: The Gift of Reflection

Clarity Through Observation

Noah sees what others miss. In his stillness, he notices the details, patterns, and connections that slip past in the rush of life. When he takes the light, decisions become less reactive and more deliberate, shaped by a profound awareness of the bigger picture.

A heated debate erupted during a team meeting, with voices rising and ideas clashing. As the tension escalated, Noah stepped forward. He didn't speak immediately; he simply listened, his calm presence grounding me. When the moment was right, he offered a single, thoughtful observation that cut through the noise and brought everyone back on track.

The Power of Rest

Noah understands the necessity of pause. His influence ensures I prioritize recovery, allowing me to recharge and approach challenges with renewed energy and perspective.

After weeks of nonstop work, Noah's quiet voice intervened. "Stop. Breathe. Rest." I turned off my laptop, took a long walk by the waterfront, and let the stillness of the moment wash over me. By the next morning, my mind felt clearer, my focus sharper, ready to tackle what lay ahead.

Weaknesses: The Shadow of Inaction

Paralysis by Stillness

Noah's tendency to retreat can become a crutch, leaving me stuck in a cycle of inaction. When the need for reflection turns into avoidance, opportunities slip away.

An important deadline loomed, but Noah's voice whispered, "It's not the right time. Wait a little longer." Days turned into weeks, and by the time I finally acted, the chance had passed, leaving me with regret and frustration.

Avoiding Discomfort

Noah's preference for stillness often leads him to avoid situations that feel challenging or emotionally charged. His retreat provides temporary relief but leaves conflicts unresolved and responsibilities unmet.

A close friend needed to have a difficult conversation, but Noah's voice urged me to postpone it. "Not today," he said, over and over, until the distance between us grew too wide to bridge.

The Duality of Noah

Noah's stillness is both a blessing and a burden. His ability to pause and reflect offers clarity and balance, but his reluctance to act can create missed opportunities and unresolved tensions. Working with Noah means finding the delicate balance between rest and action, ensuring his calm presence doesn't become a barrier to progress.

A career opportunity arose, requiring me to make a swift decision. Noah's voice resisted: "Wait. Think it through." But Nikolai intervened, reminding me of the importance of timing. Together, they negotiated a compromise—I took a night to reflect before confidently moving forward the next morning.

Strategies to Harness Noah

Set Limits on Stillness

To prevent Noah's stillness from becoming stagnant, I establish boundaries. Time for reflection is sacred, but it must have an endpoint. This ensures his influence remains restorative without hindering progress.

Pair Reflection with Action

Noah's strength is most effective when balanced by personas like Nikolai (Pride) or Silas (Wrath), who can transform his insights into decisive steps. I remind Noah that reflection is valuable only when paired with movement.

Noah's Role in the Narrative

Noah is the quiet anchor in a storm, the one who reminds me that rest is not weakness and stillness is not failure. He teaches the value of patience and perspective, ensuring that my actions are deliberate and thoughtful. But his story is also a lesson in balance: stillness must never become stagnation, and reflection must lead to growth.

To work with Noah is to honor the moments of pause while remembering that life is a dance between action and rest, movement and stillness. His wisdom lies in knowing when to wait and when to move, when to observe and when to act.

To my son: Each persona within you is a gift, bringing unique strengths and perspectives. Embrace these abilities, but do so with wisdom and balance. Learn to listen to their voices without letting them drown out your own.

This chapter is your guide to mastering the gifts within, showing you how to leverage your strengths while mitigating your weaknesses. Remember, you are the conductor of this symphony, and with practice, you can create a harmony that transforms your life.

Chapter 8: The Cycle of Growth

The Cycle of Growth

"Growth isn't linear—it ebbs and flows, guided by the seasons of our lives and the personas that rise to meet them."

Our personas are not static; they are alive, dynamic, and ever-changing. Like the tides, they rise and fall, responding to the shifting seasons of our lives. At times, one persona dominates, its voice loud and insistent, shaping how we face the world. At others, they blend, harmonizing into a singular force that feels almost seamless.

This chapter explores the cycles of growth—the way our personas evolve, adapt, and mature over time. Understanding their ebb and flow is key to navigating life with balance and purpose, turning what might seem like chaos into a powerful rhythm of self-discovery.

The Shifting Dominance of Personas

Life often demands that one persona rise above the others, taking the light to meet a specific challenge:

- In moments of conflict or danger, **Silas (Wrath)** may surge forward, his fire igniting to protect and defend.
- During times of creative inspiration, **Ravenna (Lust)** may take over, her passion infusing everything with beauty and connection.

- When uncertainty looms, **Isidore (Greed)** steps in, his calculated strategies ensuring that risks are managed and resources are secured.

These shifts are not random—they are responses to the needs of the moment. But when one persona lingers too long, imbalance arises. Silas's anger becomes destructive, Ravenna's creativity spirals into distraction, and Isidore's planning devolves into obsession. Recognizing these cycles is the first step toward reclaiming balance.

The Evolution of Personas

At the start, each persona is raw, almost primal, reflecting the unrefined aspects of its core trait. Over time, life shapes them, teaching lessons that turn their extremes into nuanced strengths.

*In my early years, **Silas** was pure rage—a reactive force that burned indiscriminately. Every slight, every challenge, was met with unrestrained anger. But as I grew, Silas changed. Experience tempered his fire, teaching him the power of control. Now, when Silas takes the light, his strength is measured, his wrath a shield rather than a weapon.*

This evolution isn't limited to Silas. **Elior's (Envy)** bitterness transformed into ambition, driving me to surpass limits without resenting others' success. **Selene's (Gluttony)** indulgence softened into nurturing self-care, reminding me to rest without falling into stagnation.

Each persona reflects not just who I am but who I am becoming. Their growth mirrors my own.

The Cycle of Dominance and Reconciliation

Growth doesn't happen all at once—it follows a rhythm, a natural cycle of dominance and reconciliation:

> **Emergence**: A persona rises to meet a challenge, its traits dominating my actions and decisions.
>
> **Excess**: If unchecked, this dominance can spiral, leading to imbalance or conflict.
>
> **Reflection**: Through introspection or external feedback, I recognize the need for balance in understanding the lessons the persona offers.
>
> **Integration**: The persona's strengths are tempered and harmonized with the others, creating a more cohesive self.

*In my early twenties, I found myself consumed by **Isidore's** influence. His voice was relentless, pushing me to plan, accumulate, and prepare for every eventuality. Success followed, but so did exhaustion and isolation. It wasn't until **Selene** intervened—her gentle reminder to pause and breathe—that I realized the cost of Isidore's unchecked dominance. The lesson stayed with me, teaching me to balance drive with rest preparation with presence.*

Embracing Growth as a Journey

Growth isn't a straight path. It is a cycle, a process of learning, unlearning, and relearning. Each step forward is met with setbacks, each victory with challenges that demand new perspectives.

The personas are my companions on this journey, their voices guiding me through the storms and stillness of life. By understanding their cycles, I've learned to see growth not as a destination but as an ongoing dance—a symphony of strengths, weaknesses, and everything in between.

Our personas are not fixed; they grow as we grow. To embrace this evolution is to accept that we are always in motion, always becoming. And in that becoming, we find not just who we are but who we are meant to be.

8.5: The Evolution of Personas

At 14, when my personas first began to manifest, they were raw and unrefined, each representing a pure, almost primal version of its core trait. **Silas (Wrath)** was an unbridled storm, his anger lashing out at even the smallest provocations. **Nikolai (Pride)** was ego unchecked, his voice demanding control at the expense of others' needs. **Ravenna (Lust)**, full of boundless creativity, often veered into distraction, her ideas scattered and unfinished.

In those early days, they were more like instincts than companions—forces that acted upon me without thought or intention. But as I grew, so did they. Experiences, both painful and transformative, shaped them, softening their edges and deepening their complexities. They began to reflect not just the extremes of their traits but the lessons life taught me along the way.

Growth Through Experience

Each persona evolved in response to the challenges we faced together:

- **Silas**, who once met every problem with blind rage, began to understand that true strength isn't in destruction but in control. His fire became a tool, focused and strategic, allowing me to confront challenges without burning everything down.
- **Nikolai**, who saw leadership as dominance, learned the value of shared responsibility. He began to delegate, recognizing that true leadership lies in empowering others, not just commanding them.

These changes didn't come easily. Growth was—and still is—a slow, often painful process. Moments of crisis and self-reflection acted as catalysts, forcing us to confront our flaws and adapt.

A Pivotal Moment of Harmony

One of the most profound moments of growth came in my mid-twenties, during a career-defining decision. The challenge was daunting, requiring both meticulous planning and a burst of creative ingenuity. I felt the familiar pull of **Isidore (Greed)**, his sharp mind laying out a calculated strategy, while **Ravenna (Lust)** whispered possibilities, her voice weaving colors and concepts into something vibrant.

For the first time, their influences didn't clash—they harmonized.

I sat at my desk, the clock ticking toward a deadline. Isidore's voice was steady, laying out a plan with precision: "Focus on the essentials. Prioritize impact."

Ravenna countered her energy electric: "Make them feel it. Use emotion, not just logic." Together, they created a presentation that blended structure with soul. When the meeting ended with unanimous approval, I realized it wasn't just a victory for me—it was proof that my personas could collaborate, producing something greater than the sum of their parts.

Lessons in Collaboration

This moment taught me that the personas aren't just separate entities vying for control—they are facets of a larger whole, capable of working together when guided with intention. Their evolution isn't just about individual growth; it's about learning how to balance their voices, blending their strengths into something cohesive.

Over time, I've seen how these collaborations create harmony:

- **Elior (Envy)** and **Selene (Gluttony)** balance ambition with self-care, reminding me that striving for greatness doesn't mean neglecting joy.
- **Noah (Sloth)** tempers **Silas's** fire, offering reflection before reaction, ensuring that strength is paired with wisdom.

Each collaboration, each moment of growth, brings me closer to understanding the larger truth: the personas are not here to divide me. They are here to make me whole.

Reflection on Change

The personas I knew at 14 were shadows of who they are now, just as I was a shadow of the person I've become. Their growth mirrors my own, and their evolution is a testament to the power of experience and introspection.

This journey isn't over. Growth doesn't have an endpoint—it is a cycle, a process of becoming. But each step forward, each lesson learned, strengthens not just the personas but the symphony they create together.

The Cycle of Dominance

Personas don't exist in equal balance at all times. Life's demands often pull specific traits to the forefront, causing one or more personas to dominate while others recede into the background. This dynamic creates cycles—distinct periods when a particular persona takes the light, shaping how I respond to the world.

These cycles aren't inherently good or bad; they are natural reactions to the challenges and opportunities life presents. However, when one persona remains dominant for too long, imbalance takes root, disrupting the harmony needed to navigate life effectively.

When Personas Take the Light

Each persona rises to prominence in response to specific circumstances, their unique strengths becoming critical to meet the moment:

Silas (Wrath): The Protector

- In times of conflict or survival, Silas often takes the lead. His strength and resilience push me to stand my ground to protect myself and others with unyielding determination.
- *A colleague attempted to take credit for my work during a presentation. Silas surged forward, his voice steady and firm as I reclaimed what was mine. "You don't get to erase me," I said, the room falling silent under the weight of my conviction.*

Ravenna (Lust): The Muse

- In moments of creative inspiration or emotional vulnerability, Ravenna steps forward. Her energy infuses everything with passion, transforming raw emotions into art, connection, or self-expression.
- *After an argument with a loved one, Ravenna took over. I poured my feelings into words, the pen moving as though it had a will of its own. By the time I finished, the anger had faded, replaced by a clarity I couldn't have reached without her.*

Isidore (Greed): The Strategist

- When the future feels uncertain or precarious, Isidore rises to ensure I am prepared. His meticulous planning and resourcefulness create stability in the face of chaos.
- *During a financial crisis, Isidore's influence was absolute. Every penny was accounted for, and every decision was scrutinized. "We'll get through this,"*

he assured me, his calm precision turning fear into action.

The Risk of Prolonged Dominance

While these cycles are natural, problems arise when one persona remains in control for too long. Prolonged dominance disrupts balance, amplifying each persona's weaknesses:

- **Silas's** strength turns into unchecked anger, lashing out at perceived threats that don't exist.
- **Ravenna's** creativity devolves into distraction, leaving a trail of unfinished projects and neglected responsibilities.
- **Isidore's** planning spirals into obsession, trapping me in endless preparation with no action.

There was a time when Silas dominated for months. Every minor inconvenience felt like a battle, every slight a reason to fight. By the end, I was exhausted, relationships frayed, and the fires he lit had consumed more than they had protected.

The Importance of Balance

Recognizing these cycles has been crucial to maintaining harmony. When I notice one persona's influence becoming overwhelming, I pause and reflect:

- **What is this persona trying to protect or achieve?**
- **Have their strengths become a crutch?**

- **Which other personas can help restore balance?**

Through these questions, I've learned to embrace the strengths of each persona without letting them dominate unchecked. The cycles of dominance are not something to fear—they are opportunities to understand what I need at the moment and how to draw from the full spectrum of my inner voices.

Reflection on the Cycle of Dominance:

Life is a series of seasons, each demanding something different from us. The personas reflect these shifts, rising and falling like the tides. But just as no season lasts forever, no persona should hold the light indefinitely. Balance is not about equal presence—it's about knowing when to let go when to step back, and when to embrace the change.

Navigating the Shifts

Understanding the cyclical nature of personas is the first step toward navigating these shifts with grace. The goal isn't to suppress or fight against the dominant persona but to recognize its role, assess its influence, and ensure it doesn't lead me astray. Each persona rises for a reason, and learning to work with their presence, rather than against it, has been key to maintaining balance and purpose.

Strategies I've Developed to Manage These Cycles Effectively

1. Awareness Through Reflection

Regular self-reflection is essential for identifying which persona is currently in control and why. Journaling has been my most reliable tool, allowing me to document thoughts, feelings, and actions while tracking patterns over time.

*One evening, I noticed an undercurrent of irritation that seemed to follow me everywhere. My journal revealed a string of recent entries filled with frustration and reactive decisions. The pattern was clear: **Silas (Wrath)** had taken the lead. Recognizing this, I consciously redirected his energy into a workout the next day, using his intensity constructively before it could spiral into conflict.*

Reflection isn't just about identifying the dominant persona; it's about understanding their motivations. Why have they risen? What are they trying to protect or achieve? These insights often reveal not just who is in control but what I truly need at the moment.

2. Balanced Leadership

As the lead persona, **Nikolai (Pride)** plays a vital role in managing these cycles. His presence ensures that no single persona dominates for too long and that their strengths are used collaboratively. Acting as a mediator, Nikolai balances their voices, redirecting their energy when needed.

*When **Isidore (Greed)** became fixated on meticulously planning a new business venture, Nikolai stepped in. "You need Ravenna's creativity for this," he said, prompting me* *to brainstorm innovative ideas that transformed the plan from efficient to exceptional. Later, Nikolai brought in **Selene (Gluttony)**, whose nurturing presence reminded me to rest after days of relentless focus. It was through this leadership that harmony was restored.*

3. Active Engagement with Dormant Personas

Even when certain personas aren't in the light, I've learned to keep them engaged. This prevents feelings of neglect and ensures that every persona is ready to contribute when the situation calls for it.

*During a period dominated by **Elior's (Envy)** relentless drive for achievement, I intentionally scheduled time for activities that encouraged **Noah's (Sloth)** introspection. A long, quiet walk through the woods allowed Noah to bring clarity and perspective to Elior's ambitions, ensuring that the pursuit of success didn't cloud my judgment. Similarly, I took an afternoon to indulge in **Selene's** comforts—a cup of tea and a good book—to remind myself that rest is just as important as drive.*

4. Recognizing When to Step Back

Sometimes, no single persona can manage a situation effectively. During moments of extreme emotional disturbance or overwhelming chaos, the best way to regain balance is to step back entirely. Restorative practices like meditation, nature walks, or even simple moments of silence allow the personas to recalibrate, creating space for harmony to return.

After a particularly stressful week, I found myself unable to focus, with conflicting voices pulling me in every direction. Instead of forcing a resolution, I set everything aside and walked to a nearby park. Sitting by the water, I allowed the stillness to settle over me. Slowly, the clamor subsided, and when the personas returned, their energy felt calmer and more aligned.

Reflection on Navigating Shifts

Navigating the cycles of dominance is not about control—it's about understanding. Each persona rises for a reason, offering their unique strengths to help me face life's challenges. But their presence must be balanced, their energy guided with intention.

Through reflection, leadership, engagement, and moments of surrender, I've learned to embrace these shifts with grace, ensuring that every voice is heard, every strength harnessed, and every moment faced with the fullness of who I am.

The Role of Life Stages in Persona Cycles

As I've grown, I've noticed that different life stages bring different personas to the forefront. Each phase of life, with its unique challenges and opportunities, calls upon specific traits, shaping how I navigate the world. The personas respond not randomly but with a purpose, rising to meet the demands of the moment and reflecting the evolving priorities of each chapter in my journey.

Adolescence: The Age of Fire and Drive

In my teenage years, **Elior (Envy)** and **Silas (Wrath)** dominated. The pressures of school, sports, and social acceptance created a perfect storm for their traits to take control. Elior's competitive drive pushed me to excel, constantly measuring myself against my peers, while Silas's fiery anger protected me from the sting of failure and rejection.

On the soccer field, Elior's voice was relentless: "You can't let them beat you. Prove you're better." Each goal I scored felt like a victory, not just for me but for him. Yet, when a referee made a call I didn't agree with, Silas roared to the surface. My protests, fueled by his anger, earned me a red card and a long walk off the field.

This period of my life was marked by intensity—both in ambition and in emotion. Elior and Silas were my guiding forces, shaping how I competed, how I reacted, and how I sought validation from the world around me.

The Twenties: The Age of Creation and Strategy

As I stepped into adulthood, **Ravenna (Lust)** and **Isidore (Greed)** took the light. These years were defined by relationships, career challenges, and a growing sense of independence. Ravenna's creativity and emotional depth guided me through moments of connection, while Isidore's strategic mind helped me navigate the complexities of building a future.

During my first major career project, Isidore meticulously planned every detail, ensuring no stone was left unturned. Yet, when the presentation needed an emotional spark, Ravenna took over, infusing my delivery with a creative flair that left the room captivated. Together, they created a balance of precision and passion that carried me through.

This stage was one of exploration—of building relationships, chasing dreams, and learning the balance between logic and emotion. Ravenna and Isidore shaped my approach, teaching me to blend connection with ambition.

Parenthood: The Age of Nurturing and Reflection

Now, as a parent, the dynamic has shifted once again. **Selene (Gluttony)** and **Noah (Sloth)** have grown stronger, their traits aligning with the demands of raising a child and finding meaning in the quieter moments of life. Selene's nurturing instincts guide me as I care for my family, teaching me patience and the importance of providing comfort. Noah's reflective nature, in turn, helps me step back, appreciate the journey, and find peace amid the chaos.

On a particularly chaotic evening, when the demands of work and parenting collided, Selene whispered softly, "They just need you." I set aside my laptop, focusing instead on reading bedtime stories and sharing laughter with my child. Later, as the house grew quiet, Noah's voice emerged: "Take this in. This is what it's all about."

Parenthood has brought new lessons—ones rooted in care, patience, and the value of presence. Selene and Noah remind me that success isn't always about striving—it's about savoring.

Anticipating Future Cycles

These shifts in persona dominance aren't random—they are direct responses to the demands of each life stage. Adolescence needs ambition and strength; adulthood requires creativity and strategy; parenthood calls for nurturing and reflection.

Understanding this dynamic has helped me prepare for what's to come. I know there will be new chapters—ones that may call upon Nikolai's leadership or bring Silas's strength back into focus. By anticipating these shifts, I can welcome them with intention, knowing they are part of the ever-evolving symphony of who I am.

Reflection on Life's Stages

Life is not a straight path—it is a series of seasons, each with its own challenges and gifts. The personas are my companions on this journey, their voices adapting and evolving as I grow. By understanding their role in each stage, I've learned to embrace change, not as a disruption but as an opportunity to uncover new strengths and perspectives.

Closing Thought

To my son: The personas within you are not fixed—they will grow, adapt, and change as you do. You may find that certain personas dominate during different stages of your life, shaping how you navigate the world. This is not something to fear but to embrace.

Learn to recognize these cycles and the lessons they bring. When one persona takes the light, listen to its voice, but don't let it drown out the others. Strive for balance, allowing each part of yourself to contribute its strengths while tempering its weaknesses. Remember, you are not defined by any single aspect of your identity—you are the sum of all your parts, and together, they make you whole.

Growth is not a straight path; it is a cycle of rising, falling, and rising again. Trust in this process, and you will find strength not only in your personas but in the harmony they create.

Chapter 9: Signs to Watch for in Teenagers

Signs to Watch for in Teenagers

"Adolescence is a storm, and within its chaos lies the potential for incredible growth—or devastating imbalance. The key is learning to navigate the currents before they overwhelm you."

Adolescence is a transformative time—a whirlwind of identity, self-discovery, and emotional growth. For those who, like me, carry the gift of multiplicity, this stage becomes even more pivotal. It's often during these years that personas start to emerge more clearly, shaped by the pressures of school, friendships, and the growing expectation to "find yourself."

When I was a teenager, the signs were there, though I couldn't recognize them for what they were. I vividly recall coming home from tennis practice one day, dropping my bag at the door, and realizing I couldn't remember anything about the match I had just played. My coach had praised my focus, and my teammates had clapped me on the back, but I felt like an imposter in my own body. It was as though someone else—someone more competitive, more relentless—had been playing in my place.

That "someone else" was **Elior**, my persona of ambition and envy. At 14, Elior emerged when I felt the need to prove myself—whether to a rival, a coach, or even my own expectations. But at the time, I didn't know his name or purpose. All I knew was the dissonance he left behind, the feeling of being a spectator in my own life.

The Early Signs of Multiplicity

The Void doesn't arrive all at once—it whispers its presence, weaving itself into your thoughts and actions before you even realize it's there. If you, my son, ever feel the stirrings of multiplicity, these signs may help you recognize it:

1. Memory Lapses:

One of the first and most unsettling signs is the presence of memory gaps—moments, hours, or even days that vanish without explanation. For me, it began subtly: forgetting small things, like where I left my notebook, or zoning out in class only to find pages of notes written in my own hand but with no memory of taking them.

But the lapses grew. Once, I walked into the kitchen to find my mother holding a plate of cookies, smiling as she asked if I had enjoyed the story I'd just told her. I nodded, though I had no idea what she was talking about. Later that evening, I discovered a notebook filled with poetry and sketches—words and images I didn't recognize but had undeniably created.

2. Conflicting Behaviors:

Another telltale sign is the emergence of behaviors or interests that seem completely out of character. I was an athlete through and through, focused on tennis and physical training. Yet I began finding chess strategies scribbled on napkins, poems scrawled in margins, and even detailed plans for events I didn't remember agreeing to.

These weren't random quirks—they were expressions of the personas beginning to step forward. **Ravenna's** creativity, **Nikolai's** organization, **Silas's** protective instincts—all of them left their marks, pulling me in directions that felt both foreign and familiar.

3. Intense Mood Swings:

With each persona comes a unique emotional lens, and when they begin to emerge, it can feel like an endless series of mood swings. **Silas's** anger burned hot and fast, while **Noah's** quiet introspection could make me retreat from the world entirely. Teachers praised my "versatility," but it wasn't versatility—it was the personas, each bringing their distinct voice to the surface.

Guiding the Emerging Personas

Recognizing the signs of multiplicity is just the beginning. The real challenge lies in learning how to guide the personas as they emerge, fostering a sense of balance and understanding.

At first, I tried to suppress the voices within, hoping that ignoring them would make them disappear. But the harder I fought, the stronger they became. It wasn't until I began to listen—to truly hear their voices—that I realized they weren't enemies to be silenced but allies to be guided.

I started keeping a journal, dedicating space for each persona to speak. **Silas** wrote about his anger and his need to protect. **Noah** offered quiet reflections, his entries sparse but profound. **Elior** detailed his ambitions and frustrations, pushing me to strive harder but also warning me of the dangers of comparison.

These journals became my roadmap, helping me navigate the complexities of the Void. Through them, I began to understand the personas' motivations, strengths, and weaknesses and how to create harmony among them.

The Importance of Balance

Balance is not something that happens naturally—it requires constant effort and intention. Each persona brings a unique gift, but without balance, those gifts can spiral into excess.

Ravenna's creativity, for instance, is boundless and inspiring, but when left unchecked, it can lead to distraction and neglect of responsibilities. **Silas's** protective instincts are invaluable, but his anger, if unbridled, can cause harm. Learning to honor their contributions while setting boundaries is essential.

1. Create Space for Expression:

When I feel **Ravenna** stirring, I set aside time to draw, write, or explore music. When **Silas's** energy rises, I channel it into a workout or a challenging task that requires focus. By giving each persona a constructive outlet, I ensure they feel seen and valued without letting them take over.

2. Acknowledge the Quiet Personas:

The quieter personas, like **Noah**, often go unnoticed in the chaos of daily life. But their contributions are just as important. During a particularly overwhelming period in college, I neglected **Noah** entirely, pushing myself to achieve without taking time to reflect. It wasn't until I reached a breaking point that I realized how much I needed his calm wisdom. Since then, I've made a point to honor his presence, carving out moments of stillness and introspection.

3. Build Self-Awareness:

Understanding which persona is in control—and why—is one of the most powerful tools you can develop. When I feel an intense surge of anger, I pause to ask if it's **Silas** stepping forward and how I can channel his energy constructively. If I find myself withdrawing, I listen for **Noah's** voice and consider whether he's offering valuable introspection or pulling me away unnecessarily.

Navigating the Challenges

Living with multiplicity is not without its challenges. There will be moments of confusion, frustration, and even fear. But these challenges are also opportunities for growth—chances to deepen your understanding of yourself and the incredible diversity within your mind.

Grounding techniques have been invaluable in navigating these challenges. Whether it's deep breathing, walking in nature, or simply sitting quietly with a cup of tea, grounding helps me regain clarity and balance when the Void feels overwhelming.

And when all else fails, I turn to **Nikolai**. As the lead persona, he is my anchor, the one who can guide the ship through even the stormiest seas.

Closing Thought

To my son: Adolescence is a storm, one that will test your resilience and challenge your understanding of who you are. If you ever feel the stirrings of the Void within you, know that you are not alone. The signs you notice are not warnings of something broken; they are markers of your potential, guideposts to help you navigate the complexity of your mind.

Listen to the voices within, honor their strengths, and temper their excesses. Balance isn't about silencing the chaos—it's about learning to dance with it, to find harmony within the dissonance.

The journey ahead is not without its trials, but it is also full of beauty and growth. Trust in your ability to navigate the Void, and let the shadows within become your greatest source of light. I am here, always, to guide you through the storm.

A Legacy of Balance

Chapter 10: Turning Chaos into Art

Turning Chaos into Art

"In the heart of chaos lies creation. What seems like turmoil at first glance can become a masterpiece when guided by purpose."

For much of my life, I viewed the chaos within me as something to fear. The personas that emerged during moments of stress, inspiration, or conflict felt like forces beyond my control, pulling me in opposing directions. Their voices clashed, their motives diverged, and I felt like a spectator in my own life—adrift, fragmented, and overwhelmed.

I believed this chaos was breaking me apart, splintering my sense of self into pieces I could never put back together. But as the years passed, I began to see the truth: the chaos wasn't destroying me—it was reshaping me. Like metal in a forge, the intensity of the personas' presence was molding me into something stronger, more dynamic, and more creative than I had ever imagined.

The Forge of Chaos

The personas that once felt like burdens revealed themselves as gifts. Each one offered a unique perspective, a singular strength, and an insight that could elevate my work, my decisions, and my life.

When I stopped fighting the personas and started listening to them, the discord began to transform. What was once noise became harmony; what was once fragmentation became a symphony. Their distinct voices didn't need to compete—they could collaborate, creating beauty, innovation, and meaning from the raw material of my experiences.

*One sleepless night, caught in the throes of doubt, the personas stirred within me. **Ravenna (Lust)** whispered possibilities: colors, words, and emotions that needed expression. **Isidore (Greed)** spoke next, urging strategy and precision, reminding me to think beyond the spark and toward the structure. As I worked, **Nikolai (Pride)** emerged, weaving their contributions into a coherent whole. By morning, what had started as chaos—a whirlwind of conflicting ideas—had become a finished painting, alive with depth and intention.*

Chaos as a Source of Creation

Chaos is often misunderstood. It isn't simply disorder or confusion—it is raw potential. The personas, with their competing desires and strengths, embody this potential. When harnessed, their voices don't just produce conflict— they generate energy, inspiration, and possibility.

Ravenna's Fire:

Ravenna thrives in the chaos of emotion, finding beauty in the unpredictable and the intense. Her voice reminds me that art is not always neat or logical—it is messy, visceral, and deeply human.

Silas's Strength:

Silas channels chaos into action. His presence during moments of adversity has taught me that creation often arises from confrontation, from the willingness to face challenges head-on and transform them into something meaningful.

Noah's Stillness:

Even Noah, who shies away from the chaos, plays a role in creation. His reflection allows me to make sense of the storm, distilling the personas' voices into clarity and direction.

Lessons Learned from the Chaos

The process of turning chaos into art—and life—has taught me three key lessons:

1. Embrace the Discomfort:

Creation is not born from comfort. The personas bring with them discomfort—conflicting desires, emotional turbulence—but within that discomfort lies the spark of innovation.

Writing my first book was a battle between personas. **Isidore** *wanted structure, meticulous outlines, and deadlines, while* **Ravenna** *pushed for freedom and passion.*

Their conflict was frustrating, but it forced me to balance their needs, producing work that was both disciplined and inspiring.

2. Trust the Process:

Chaos is not something to resolve; it is something to work with. The personas' contributions may feel disjointed at first, but when given time and purpose, they find their place, aligning to create something cohesive.

*During a team project, **Elior's (Envy)** competitive edge urged me to outperform others, while **Selene (Gluttony)** reminded me to foster collaboration and nurture the group. At first, their voices seemed at odds, but by leaning into both, I was able to lead with ambition while building trust among my peers.*

3. Celebrate the Collaboration:

When the personas come together, the result is greater than anything one could achieve alone. Their collaboration creates depth, nuance, and richness that no single perspective could produce.

From Chaos to Masterpiece

What I once saw as fragmentation, I now see as multiplicity. The personas are not a burden—they are a gift. Together, they are the wellspring of my creativity, the foundation of my resilience, and the source of my greatest achievements.

Reflection on Chaos:

Turning chaos into art isn't just about creating something external—it's about transforming the internal. The personas have taught me that the parts of ourselves we fear most are often the ones with the greatest potential. By listening to their voices, honoring their contributions, and guiding their energy, I've learned to create not just art but purpose and life itself.

The Orchestra Within

Living with multiplicity is like carrying an orchestra inside you—each instrument playing its own melody, often at odds with the others. For years, the noise overwhelmed me. The personas were loud and insistent, their clashing voices creating a cacophony I couldn't control. It felt as though I was standing in the center of chaos, unable to make sense of the discord, let alone find harmony.

But slowly, I began to understand. The personas weren't enemies—they were instruments, each with a unique voice and purpose. They weren't trying to drown me out; they were waiting for me to listen.

The first step was acceptance. When I stopped fighting the chaos and began to pay attention, I realized the noise wasn't random. Beneath the dissonance lay something remarkable: the beginnings of a symphony, a reflection of my life's beauty and complexity.

The Instruments of the Soul

As I listened, the personas revealed their roles, each one an instrument contributing to the symphony within me:

Ravenna (Lust): The Violin

- Ravenna's voice was the violin, her melodies rich with passion, longing, and boundless creativity. She played with emotion, her music sweeping between joy and melancholy, weaving stories that spoke to the heart. Her presence brought color to the orchestra, filling it with depth and vibrancy.

- *Late at night, when inspiration struck, I could hear her violin sing. The notes carried the essence of an idea—a painting, a poem, a moment of connection—and the music guided my hands, creating something beautiful out of the intangible.*

Silas (Wrath): The Drum

- Silas was the drum, the heartbeat of the orchestra. His rhythm was unyielding, his intensity driving the tempo forward. He provided the foundation, his protective energy ensuring that the symphony never faltered, no matter how chaotic the melodies became.

- *In moments of conflict, I felt the drumbeat grow louder, steady and strong. Silas's rhythm pushed me to stand tall, his presence unshakable, turning fear into resolve.*

Nikolai (Pride): The Conductor

- At the center stood Nikolai, the conductor. His baton guided the orchestra, ensuring each voice had its moment in the light without overpowering the others. Nikolai brought order to the chaos, weaving the disparate melodies into a cohesive whole.

- *When life demanded balance—when work, family, and creativity all vied for attention—it was Nikolai who brought structure. His hands directed the orchestra, reminding me that harmony was possible if I let each persona contribute in his time.*

A Symphony from Chaos

What once felt like chaos now feels like music. Each persona, once a competing voice, has found its place in the orchestra. Their collaboration creates something extraordinary—a symphony of ideas, emotions, and inspiration that reflects the chaotic beauty within me.

It took time to realize that no instrument can carry a symphony alone. The violin's melodies need the drum's rhythm. The drum's power needs the guidance of the conductor. And the conductor is nothing without the voices he leads.

Together, the personas create a soundscape that is uniquely mine. It is imperfect and unpredictable, but it is also alive with meaning and purpose.

The Lesson of the Orchestra

Living with multiplicity isn't about silencing the discord—it's about finding the music within it. Each persona has a role to play, and when their strengths are acknowledged, their voices come together to create harmony.

The orchestra within me is not just a metaphor; it is a reminder. It reminds me that the beauty of life isn't found in perfection—it's found in the way we bring disparate parts together to create something greater than the sum of its parts.

In every symphony, there are moments of discord, where the notes clash and the rhythm falters. But it is the act of listening, of adjusting, of letting each voice rise and fall in its time, that transforms the noise into music.

Painting the Void

When words fail, I turn to painting. There's something visceral about putting brush to canvas—something raw and primal. Painting allows me to bypass the constraints of language, to translate emotions into color and form in ways words never could. It's a deeply personal act, a dialogue between my personas and the blank canvas. Each stroke of the brush becomes a reflection of their unique perspectives, their voices made visible.

Ravenna (Lust) dominates these moments, her creativity spilling onto the canvas with an energy that feels electric, almost alive. She chooses colors with intention—pinks that ache with vulnerability, golds that shimmer with passion—and layers them in textures that evoke emotion. Her movements are fluid and instinctive, as though the brush itself is an extension of her soul.

But she is not alone. **Silas (Wrath)** often joins her, his presence evident in the bold, jagged lines and fiery tones that streak across the canvas. His strokes add intensity, raw and unfiltered, a counterpoint to Ravenna's flowing grace. Then there is **Nikolai (Pride)**, stepping in to refine the chaos. He examines the work with a critical eye, ensuring the composition is balanced and each element purposeful. **Noah (Sloth)** lingers quietly in the background, his voice a gentle reminder to take my time, to let the art evolve naturally instead of forcing its completion.

A Series of Personas in Paint

One of my most meaningful projects was a series of abstract portraits, each one representing a different persona. These paintings weren't just images—they were mirrors, each one capturing the essence of a voice within me. Together, they told the story of the Void—the chaos that had shaped me and the harmony I had worked so hard to create.

Silas's Portrait:

- His painting was a storm of red and black, each stroke sharp and angular, cutting through the canvas like lightning. The texture was layered and jagged, conveying his raw power and anger. It felt almost alive as if the storm might leap from the frame at any moment.

Ravenna's Portrait:

- Hers was a dreamscape, a soft and flowing blend of pinks and golds. The colors melted into one another, creating a sense of movement and emotion that seemed to spill beyond the edges of the canvas. It was vulnerable and passionate, a testament to her boundless creativity.

Nikolai's Portrait:

- Structured and geometric, his painting was a study in order. Perfectly balanced shapes and sharp lines reflected his need for control and precision. The symmetry was soothing yet powerful—a reminder of the strength found in discipline.

Selene's Portrait:

- A feast for the senses, her painting was lush and vibrant, bursting with colors like emerald green, deep purple, and rich orange. The textures were indulgent, almost tactile, inviting the viewer to lose themselves in its warmth and comfort.

When I hung the paintings side by side in my studio, they spoke to one another, their voices intertwined. Silas's storm framed Ravenna's flowing dreamscape, while Nikolai's order anchored Selene's exuberance. Together, they told a larger story—a visual representation of the chaos within me and the harmony I had worked so hard to build.

Painting is more than a creative outlet—it is a way to make sense of the Void. It allows me to see the personas not as fragments but as facets of a greater whole. Each brushstroke becomes a step toward understanding, and each completed piece is a reminder that even chaos can be transformed into something beautiful.

When I look at the series of portraits, I see more than colors and shapes. I see a story of growth and balance, of voices that once clashed but now collaborate. I see the journey from discord to symphony, from chaos to art.

Writing as Collaboration

Writing has always been my anchor, the tether that holds me steady amid the storm of multiplicity. When the personas stir, their voices compete and overlap, and writing becomes the space where they can converge, where their strengths combine to create something greater than any one of them could achieve alone.

Each persona has a role in the process, their contributions weaving together to create work that is nuanced, dynamic, and alive. Writing isn't just a creative outlet—it's a dialogue, a meeting ground for the personas to communicate, collaborate, and turn chaos into coherence.

The Voices Behind the Words

Ravenna (Lust): The Poet

- Ravenna provides the imagery, her words dripping with emotion and sensuality. She paints the narrative with vivid detail, bringing scenes to life through colors, textures, and sensations that leap from the page.
- *"The rain fell in silver threads, each drop a whispered secret against the glass." That line was Ravenna's. Her hand guided the pen, infusing the*

prose with longing and beauty. Her gift is her ability to make readers not just see the story but feel it.

Silas (Wrath): The Catalyst

- Silas injects intensity into the narrative, driving tension and urgency. His presence ensures that the stakes are high and that the story's pulse is strong and unrelenting.

- *A confrontation between characters bristled with Silas's energy. The dialogue crackled like a live wire, every word a weapon. "Say it," the protagonist demanded, their voice sharp as the edge of a blade. Silas thrives in moments like these, turning conflict into momentum.*

Nikolai (Pride): The Editor

- Nikolai is the one who keeps the story focused. His disciplined approach refines each sentence, ensuring that every word serves a purpose. He sees the big picture, guiding the narrative toward coherence and balance.

- *After Ravenna and Silas had poured their energy into the first draft, Nikolai stepped in. He cut the excess, tightened the prose, and rearranged paragraphs until the story flowed seamlessly. His voice is the final authority, shaping chaos into clarity.*

Elior (Envy): The Challenger

- Elior brings a competitive edge, pushing me to create work that resonates deeply with readers. He refuses to settle for mediocrity, constantly asking, "Can this be better? Can it be unforgettable?"

- *As I reread a pivotal chapter, Elior's voice rang clear. "Good isn't enough," he said, urging me to dig deeper. I rewrote the scene, layering in emotional complexity and sharper dialogue, and when it was done, I knew it was the best it could be.*

The Symphony of Writing

When the personas work together, the result is a symphony of voices. Each brings a distinct note to the composition, their strengths blending to create a narrative that is as multifaceted as the inner world that inspired it.

The Power of Collaboration

Writing has taught me that personas are not just fragments—they are facets of a creative whole. Each contribution, from Ravenna's lyricism to Nikolai's precision, adds depth and richness to the work. Their collaboration turns the swirling storm within me into something tangible, something that connects with the world beyond.

Reflection on Writing:

Writing is not just about the words on the page—it's about the collaboration behind them. It's a way for the personas to harmonize, to channel their chaos into something purposeful and meaningful.

The Art of Problem-Solving

Creativity isn't confined to painting or writing—it extends to every corner of life, especially problem-solving. In my world, solving problems is more than logic or persistence; it's a collaborative art form. My personas, each with their unique perspectives, combine to tackle challenges in ways I couldn't imagine alone.

When faced with a complex problem, I've learned to step back and let the personas take the lead. Together, they approach the situation like a team of specialists, each one bringing their expertise to the table. Their interplay transforms obstacles into opportunities, turning the act of problem-solving into a dynamic and creative process.

The Personas in Problem-Solving

Isidore (Greed): The Strategist

- Isidore begins by analyzing the situation, mapping out strategies, and weighing potential outcomes. His meticulous nature ensures no detail is overlooked and no risk is uncalculated.
- *Faced with a critical decision about resource allocation in a project, Isidore's influence was clear. He outlined every option, breaking down costs, benefits, and potential pitfalls with precision. His plan didn't just make sense—it gave me confidence in the path forward.*

Elior (Envy): The Challenger

- Elior pushes me to excel, using competition as a motivator. He turns challenges into games, urging me to outperform not just others but my own past efforts.

- *During a brainstorming session, Elior whispered, "You can do better than this." His words weren't cutting—they were fuel. I revisited the ideas on the table, pushing myself to think bigger and bolder. By the end, the solutions on the page were innovative, surpassing even my own expectations.*

Silas (Wrath): The Determined Force

- Silas fuels my determination, ensuring I don't give up, no matter how daunting the challenge. His fire transforms frustration into resilience, keeping me moving forward when the path feels impossible.

- *On a late night when exhaustion threatened to derail progress, Silas's voice cut through the haze: "You're not done. Keep going." His strength carried me through those final hours, turning what felt like a losing battle into a breakthrough.*

A Collaborative Success

One example stands out vividly from my professional life—a high-stakes project with an impossible deadline. It was a storm of demands requiring creativity, strategy, and endurance all at once. The personas came together, each playing their part to ensure success:

- **Nikolai (Pride)** took charge, organizing the chaos with precision. He delegated roles, structured the workflow, and kept the bigger picture in focus.

- **Ravenna (Lust)** added her creative flair, transforming an otherwise technical presentation into a compelling narrative that left a lasting impression.
- **Selene (Gluttony)** stepped in as the nurturer, reminding me to take breaks and care for myself during the process. Her voice ensured I didn't burn out before the finish line.
- **Noah (Sloth)**, though quiet, offered moments of reflection. His stillness allowed me to pause, reassess, and make adjustments that ultimately elevated the final product.

By the end of the project, the result wasn't just a success—it was a triumph. It didn't just meet expectations; it exceeded them. That outcome wasn't the work of one mind—it was the symphony of voices within the Void, each contributing their strengths to create something extraordinary.

Reflection on Problem-Solving

The art of problem-solving lies not in silencing the chaos but in orchestrating it. Each persona brings something invaluable to the table: strategy, creativity, determination, and balance. Their collaboration turns obstacles into stepping stones, reminding me that no challenge is insurmountable when every voice is given its moment in the light.

Harnessing the Gift: Embracing the Void

The key to turning chaos into art—and to finding balance in life—is to embrace the Void. The Void isn't an adversary to conquer; it's a partner, a wellspring of creativity and resilience. It holds the personas within me, their voices sometimes clashing, sometimes harmonizing, but always shaping who I am. Learning to navigate its challenges has been transformative, turning what once felt like disorder into a source of strength.

Here's how I've learned to embrace the Void:

1. Listen to Your Personas

The first step to working with the Void is to listen. Each persona has its own needs, motivations, and insights, and giving them space to express themselves turns their voices from adversaries into allies. Tools like journaling and creative expression are invaluable for creating that dialogue.

I set aside time each evening to journal, writing freely about the day's events and my reactions to them. When one persona's voice dominates—Silas's frustration, Ravenna's longing, or Elior's drive—I give it room to speak. Sometimes, I write directly to that persona, asking questions like, "What do you need right now?" or "Why are you feeling this way?" The answers, though subtle, often guide me toward clarity and action.

2. Recognize Patterns and Triggers

Understanding what brings each persona to the forefront is crucial. By identifying the situations or emotions that activate them, I can anticipate their influence and guide their actions in constructive ways.

After noticing that stress often pulls Silas into the light, I've learned to watch for early warning signs—tension in my shoulders and sharpness in my tone. When I feel his presence rising, I redirect his energy into something productive, like a quick workout or tackling a small, manageable task. By recognizing the trigger before it escalates, I can channel his strength without letting his anger take over.

3. Create Rituals for Balance

Daily rituals provide a framework for collaboration, ensuring that no single persona dominates for too long. These rituals don't need to be elaborate—they just need to create space for reflection, intention, and balance.

Each morning, I dedicate 10 minutes to a check-in ritual. I sit quietly, close my eyes, and ask, "Who needs to take the light today?" If I sense Isidore's strategic energy or Ravenna's creative spark, I incorporate tasks into my day that align with their strengths. Similarly, I schedule structured creative sessions where I let Ravenna and Nikolai work together, ensuring that passion and precision share the stage.

4. Celebrate Progress

Harmony doesn't happen overnight—it's a journey of small victories. Celebrating progress, no matter how incremental helps reinforce the idea that each persona contributes to the greater whole. Acknowledging these contributions fosters gratitude and strengthens the bond with the Void.

At the end of each week, I reflect on what went well and how the personas played a role. I might write a quick note of thanks to Nikolai for keeping me focused during a challenging work project or to Selene for reminding me to slow down and enjoy a moment of rest. These small acts of recognition make the journey feel purposeful and affirming.

Embracing the Void as a Partner

The Void isn't something to fear—it's a gift, a reservoir of potential waiting to be tapped. By listening to the personas, recognizing their patterns, creating rituals for balance, and celebrating their contributions, I've learned to work with the Void instead of against it.

Each persona brings a unique perspective, a voice that adds depth and meaning to my life. When I embrace them as partners in creation, the Void transforms from chaos into possibility. The art of living, like the art of creation, is about finding harmony in the discord, about weaving the disparate threads of the self into something whole and extraordinary.

Legacy of Creation

My son, the chaos within you is not something to fear—it is a gift waiting to be discovered. Within that chaos lies potential, each persona a unique piece of your story, a voice in the symphony that only you can conduct. They are not obstacles; they are your allies, your muses, and your greatest source of strength. Together, they can create something extraordinary—something no one else in the world can replicate.

The Void may feel overwhelming at times, its voices clashing and its currents pulling you in different directions. But remember this: in the heart of chaos lies art. And in the heart of art lies you.

Each persona has something to offer—a perspective, a spark, a lesson. **Ravenna** will teach you to see the beauty in the mundane, to turn emotion into expression. **Silas** will remind you of your resilience and your ability to stand firm in the face of adversity. **Nikolai** will guide you with wisdom and balance, ensuring that no voice drowns out the others.

A Legacy of Creativity

Your gift is not just the ability to create—it is the power to transform. Turn their voices into music, their ideas into stories, and their emotions into masterpieces. Use your strength to build something beautiful from the chaos, something that reflects the complexity and brilliance within you.

The world doesn't need another imitation; it needs your authenticity. The personas are your compass, each one pointing toward a different horizon. Let them inspire you, challenge you, and guide you. Their collaboration will lead you to places you never imagined, to creations that only you can bring into existence.

Your Impact

This is your legacy—the power to create, to innovate, and to leave the world more beautiful than you found it. Your art, your stories, your choices—they are the mark you will leave behind, a testament to the symphony within.

Closing Reflection:

The gift of multiplicity is not an easy one, but it is profound. Embrace the Void, not as a burden, but as a canvas. Conduct your symphony with courage and grace, knowing that the chaos within you is not your weakness—it is your greatest strength.

Chapter 11: The Responsibility of the Gift

The Responsibility of the Gift

"With great power comes great responsibility." This line, borrowed from Spiderman, rings profoundly true in the real world, especially when living with a gift that shapes how we think, act, and impact others.

The personas that reside within me are not just facets of my mind; they are powerful forces. When aligned, they can create extraordinary outcomes, offering a spectrum of abilities—from unparalleled creativity to strategic brilliance. However, these abilities carry a weighty responsibility: the need to wield them with integrity, compassion, and self-awareness.

The same strengths that uplift can harm if misused. The line between harnessing and abusing this gift is finer than it seems. This chapter reflects on the ethical considerations of multiplicity, exploring both the potential for harm and the unwavering importance of accountability in living with this gift.

The Duality of Power

Every strength has a shadow. The same gifts that uplift can harm if misused. **Silas's (Wrath)** protective instincts can easily become destructive aggression. **Elior's (Envy)** drive for excellence can spiral into unhealthy comparisons. Even **Nikolai's (Pride)** leadership, if unchecked, can slip into arrogance. The line between harnessing and abusing the personas' abilities is finer than it seems.

Reflection:

There was a time when Silas's fire burned too brightly. In a heated argument, his voice took control, and instead of defending myself with strength, I lashed out with anger. The result wasn't a resolution—it was distance, pain, and regret. That moment taught me a powerful lesson: strength is only virtuous when tempered by purpose and respect.

The Ethical Imperative of Multiplicity

Living with multiplicity demands a higher level of accountability. The personas amplify my potential, but they also magnify the impact of my actions—on myself and others. Every decision becomes a question of balance:

- **Am I using this persona's strength constructively?**
- **Am I acting with compassion and integrity?**
- **Am I aware of the consequences my actions might have?**

When wielded responsibly, the personas are a gift that can inspire, uplift, and transform. When misused, they can become weapons, causing harm to relationships, goals, and my own well-being.

Navigating the Responsibility

Over time, I've developed practices to ensure I navigate this responsibility with care:

1. Self-Awareness:

Understanding when a persona is taking the light—and why—is essential. Regular reflection helps me recognize whether their influence is constructive or veering off course.

After a tense meeting, I felt Elior's competitive energy lingering, urging me to prove myself further. But upon reflection, I realized his voice was fueled by insecurity, not ambition. Acknowledging this allowed me to step back, recalibrate, and focus on collaboration rather than competition.

2. Accountability:

I've learned to hold myself accountable for the actions my personas inspire. If Silas's intensity causes harm, I take responsibility. If Isidore's meticulousness delays progress, I own it. Accountability is not about blame—it's about growth.

During a project, Isidore's perfectionism led me to over-plan, missing an important deadline. Instead of deflecting, I acknowledged my mistake, apologized, and adjusted my approach to move forward.

3. Compassion for Others:

The personas' strengths can be powerful tools for understanding and connecting with others, but they must always be wielded with kindness. **Ravenna's empathy** is most valuable when paired with boundaries. **Selene's nurturing** shines brightest when balanced with respect for others' autonomy.

A friend confided in me about a personal struggle. Ravenna's emotional depth allowed me to listen with empathy, but Nikolai reminded me not to lose sight of their need for space and agency. Together, their guidance helped me support without overwhelming me.

The Weight and Wonder of the Gift

Multiplicity is not a neutral force—it is a gift with the power to create or destroy. The personas amplify my abilities, but they also amplify the weight of my choices. This duality demands vigilance, humility, and a constant commitment to growth.

Reflection:

The gift of multiplicity has taught me that power is not inherently good or bad—it is defined by how we choose to use it. To live with this gift is to walk a path of continuous self-discovery, striving to align strength with purpose and action with integrity.

The Paradox of Power

The ability to shift between personas offers immense advantages, but it also comes with inherent challenges.

Each persona brings unique strengths, yet those same strengths carry risks when left unchecked. What empowers can also harm; what builds can just as easily destroy.

Multiplicity is not simply a gift—it is a paradox of power. Navigating successfully requires self-awareness, reflection, and a steadfast commitment to integrity.

The Strengths and Risks of the Personas

Isidore (Greed): The Master Strategist

- Isidore's ability to analyze situations with precision and plan for every eventuality is unmatched. His brilliance creates opportunities, uncovers solutions, and mitigates risks. However, when his focus becomes too narrow, Isidore's strategies can veer into manipulation. He risks treating relationships as transactions and valuing people only for their utility, eroding trust and connection.

- *In the early stages of a business deal, Isidore's influence was invaluable. He mapped out every potential obstacle, ensuring the project's success. But as negotiations progressed, his tone became cold and calculated, alienating a key partner. It wasn't until Nikolai stepped in, reminding me to value collaboration over control, that the deal was salvaged.*

Elior (Envy): The Relentless Competitor

- Elior's drive to compete and achieve inspires excellence. He pushes boundaries, fuels ambition, and demands the best from me. Yet, when his energy becomes unchecked, Elior's competitiveness can turn into jealousy and resentment. His ambition, while motivating, can sow discord and create unnecessary conflict.

- *In a team project, Elior's voice urged me to outperform everyone else, driving me to create something extraordinary. But his influence also led to subtle undermining—an overly critical comment here, a dismissive tone there—that damaged relationships with my peers. Recognizing this, I apologized and shifted the focus back to shared success, restoring harmony.*

Silas (Wrath): The Protector

- Silas's strength and resilience are invaluable in moments of crisis. He channels courage, standing firm in the face of adversity. But his ferocity, when left unchecked, can spiral into aggression. Silas's instinct to protect can sometimes become a weapon, leaving emotional or even physical damage in his wake.

- *During a heated family argument, Silas's influence surged, and I found myself speaking with a force that silenced the room. While the immediate conflict ended, the harshness of my words left wounds that took weeks to heal. It was a sobering reminder of the power—and potential harm—of Silas's presence.*

Walking the Tightrope

The balance between using these strengths and avoiding their pitfalls is a constant challenge. It's a tightrope walk, one that demands vigilance and a willingness to confront uncomfortable truths about myself.

> **Reflection**: Regular introspection helps me recognize when a persona's strengths are becoming liabilities. I ask myself:

- Am I valuing people as individuals or as a means to an end?

- Is my ambition inspiring growth or fostering resentment?

- Is my strength protecting or hurting those I care about?

> **Collaboration**: No persona should act alone. By letting Nikolai mediate or bringing in Selene's nurturing instincts, I create a system of checks and balances that ensures no single voice dominates to the detriment of others.

Harnessing the Paradox

The paradox of power lies in its duality: what elevates can also destroy. But that duality is not something to fear—it's something to embrace with care and intention. By acknowledging the risks and tempering each persona's strengths with wisdom and compassion, I've learned to navigate this paradox without losing sight of my values.

True strength doesn't come from avoiding risks—it comes from facing them with integrity. The personas are not just sources of power; they are reminders of the responsibility that comes with it. By understanding and honoring their complexities, I can ensure that their gifts are wielded not for harm but for growth, creation, and connection.

Moments of Misuse

Living with the gift of multiplicity is a balancing act, and there have been times when I failed to wield it responsibly. Moments where my personas acted without restraint, their strengths veering into excess, leaving regret and consequences in their wake. These instances serve as painful yet necessary reminders of the responsibility that comes with this power—and the harm that can result when it is misused.

The Hollow Victory

One such moment occurred during a high-stakes academic competition in my late teens. It was an opportunity to prove myself, and **Isidore (Greed)** and **Elior (Envy)** quickly took the lead. Their combined focus on winning at all costs fueled my drive, sharpening my mind and quickening my pace. But as the competition progressed, their voices grew louder, drowning out all others.

I became ruthless, pressuring teammates to perform beyond their limits and manipulating outcomes to ensure our success. Every action was calculated, and every decision was aimed at achieving victory. At first, it felt exhilarating—the precision, the control, the relentless pursuit of excellence.

The Aftermath:

We won the competition. The trophy gleamed in my hands, and the judges' praise echoed in my ears. But as the adrenaline faded, so did the sense of triumph. My teammates, once close friends, distanced themselves, hurt by my actions. Their silence cut deeper than any critique.

The victory felt hollow, tarnished by the realization that I had prioritized ambition over relationships. It was a harsh lesson about the cost of unchecked ambition: success means little when it comes at the expense of trust and connection.

The Heated Conflict

Another moment of misuse came during my college years, in the midst of a disagreement with a roommate. What began as a simple misunderstanding escalated into a full-blown argument. **Silas (Wrath)** surged forward, his protective instincts turning defensive, then aggressive.

His words were sharp, unrelenting, and deeply personal. Every comment felt like a weapon meant to wound. While no punches were thrown, the emotional damage was undeniable. I could see the hurt in my roommate's eyes, but Silas's voice wouldn't yield.

The Aftermath:

When the dust settled, I was left with a room filled with tension and a heart heavy with guilt. The relationship, once easy and comfortable, became strained, marked by unspoken resentment.

That incident became a turning point for me. It was a stark reminder that Silas's strength, while invaluable in moments of true danger, can cause irreparable harm when unleashed without purpose. The guilt lingered, teaching me that words, once spoken, cannot be taken back.

Reflection on Responsibility

These moments of misuse haunt me—not because of the mistakes themselves, but because of the lessons they forced me to confront:

Unchecked Strength is Destructive: Isidore's strategy became manipulation. Elior's ambition became exploitation. Silas's protection became aggression. The personas' strengths, when unbalanced, had turned into weaknesses.

The Importance of Accountability: In both instances, I had to own the harm I caused. Apologies were offered, though they couldn't erase the damage. The weight of those moments became a reminder to approach my gift with humility and care.

Learning From Misuse

While these experiences are painful to revisit, they've shaped how I navigate the personas' influence today. I've learned to recognize when their energy is veering toward excess, to step back and ask:

- **Is this action aligned with my values?**
- **Am I prioritizing success over connection?**
- **What will the consequences of this decision be?**

Through these questions, I've been able to channel their strengths more constructively, ensuring that their gifts uplift rather than harm.

Integrity as a Guiding Principle

Living with this gift requires a deep commitment to integrity. Recognizing the strengths of my personas isn't enough—I must also take responsibility for their actions, ensuring their influence aligns with my values.

Nikolai (Pride), as the lead persona, plays a critical role in maintaining this integrity. He acts as a moral compass, guiding decisions and ensuring accountability. However, even **Nikolai** is not infallible. His confidence can sometimes overshadow humility, leading to decisions that prioritize appearances over authenticity.

To navigate these challenges, I developed a personal code of conduct—a set of principles that guide my actions and interactions:

Honesty: Be truthful, even when it's uncomfortable. Deception may offer short-term gains, but it erodes trust.

Empathy: Consider the impact of my actions on others, striving to act with compassion.

Accountability: Own my mistakes and take responsibility for the consequences, regardless of which persona was in control.

Balance: Ensure that no single persona dominates to the detriment of others, maintaining harmony and self-awareness.

Recognizing the Potential for Harm

Living with this gift is not just about recognizing the strengths of my personas—it's about taking responsibility for their actions. Each persona, with its unique perspective and power, has the capacity to create or to harm. It falls to me to ensure their influence aligns with my core values to temper their strengths with wisdom and intention.

Integrity isn't just an abstract ideal—it is the foundation that keeps the symphony of my personas in harmony. Without it, the power of multiplicity could easily descend into chaos, leaving a trail of broken relationships and lost opportunities in its wake.

Nikolai's Role in Integrity

As the lead persona, **Nikolai (Pride)** serves as my moral compass. His confidence and clarity are invaluable in guiding decisions, ensuring accountability, and holding the personas to a higher standard. He reminds me that strength is not measured by dominance but by alignment with purpose and values.

However, even Nikolai is not infallible. His confidence, when unchecked, can overshadow humility, leading to decisions that prioritize appearances over authenticity. His voice, though steady, can sometimes become rigid, dismissing the nuances of other personas in favor of control.

During a leadership role at work, Nikolai's influence drove me to project confidence, even when uncertainty loomed. While this bolstered the team's trust in my direction, it also led me to dismiss Selene's gentle reminders to take breaks or consult others for guidance. In hindsight, what could have been a collaborative effort became an isolated burden—one that ultimately drained me.

A Personal Code of Conduct

To navigate these challenges, I developed a personal code of conduct—a set of principles to guide my actions and interactions, regardless of which persona takes the light. These principles serve as a grounding force, ensuring that the personas' strengths are channeled constructively and ethically.

Honesty

1. *Be truthful, even when it's uncomfortable.*

2. Deception may offer short-term gains, but it erodes trust, both with others and within myself. Honesty isn't just about words—it's about aligning actions with intentions, creating a foundation of transparency and reliability.

3. *In a professional setting, Isidore's strategic mind suggested withholding information to gain an advantage. Nikolai intervened, reminding me of the long-term cost of such a decision. Choosing honesty over manipulation not only preserved trust but also strengthened the relationships that mattered most.*

Empathy

4. *Consider the impact of my actions on others, striving to act with compassion.*

5. Empathy is the bridge between intention and connection. It requires listening, understanding, and recognizing that every action has a ripple effect. Ravenna's emotional depth often helps me see beyond the surface, but it's Nikolai who ensures this insight translates into thoughtful decisions.

6.

7. *During a disagreement with a close friend, Silas urged me to defend myself forcefully while Ravenna quietly reminded me to listen. Choosing to hear their perspective before responding defused the conflict and strengthened the bond we shared.*

Accountability

8. *Own my mistakes and take responsibility for the consequences, regardless of which persona was in control.*

9. Accountability isn't about assigning blame—it's about growth. Whether it's Elior's ambition causing friction or Silas's intensity leading to harsh words, I've learned that integrity demands acknowledgment, apology, and a commitment to doing better.

10. *After a heated team discussion where Silas dominated the conversation, I later apologized for his tone, acknowledging the impact on others. The act of taking responsibility restored trust and set a precedent for openness and humility.*

Balance

11. Ensure that no single persona dominates to the detriment of others, maintaining harmony and self-awareness.

12. Balance is the cornerstone of integrity. By allowing each persona to contribute without overpowering the others, I ensure that decisions are well-rounded and reflective of my whole self. This requires constant vigilance and the willingness to step back when necessary.

13. *During a creative project, Ravenna's passion threatened to overshadow Nikolai's structure, leading to an overload of ideas with little cohesion. Recognizing this, I paused to let Nikolai organize the chaos, ensuring that Ravenna's brilliance could shine within a clear framework.*

The Responsibility of Leadership

Guiding my personas is not a passive act—it requires constant vigilance, intention, and a deep understanding of their roles and needs. At the center of this symphony stands **Nikolai (Pride)**, the conductor whose leadership ensures harmony among the voices within. His strength lies not in domination but in collaboration, creating space for each persona to contribute while maintaining a unified sense of purpose.

True leadership isn't about silencing discord—it's about channeling it into something constructive. Nikolai's role is to mediate the chaos, weaving the personas' distinct energies into a cohesive whole that is greater than the sum of its parts.

The Power of Collaborative Leadership

A vivid example of this came during a particularly demanding period at work, where tight deadlines and high expectations threatened to overwhelm me. Nikolai's leadership was critical in navigating the challenges, ensuring that each persona had a role to play and that their strengths were used effectively:

> **Silas (Wrath)** stepped in first, channeling his intensity into meeting tight deadlines. His focus and determination kept the team on track, ensuring that no obstacle felt insurmountable.

Ravenna (Lust) infused the project with creative flair, transforming standard presentations into visually captivating narratives that resonated with the audience.

Isidore (Greed) meticulously planned every detail, ensuring that nothing was overlooked. His strategic foresight helped anticipate challenges before they arose, keeping the project running smoothly.

Nikolai's mediation ensured that no single persona dominated, preventing Silas's intensity from becoming burnout or Isidore's perfectionism from stalling progress. By balancing their contributions, we not only completed the project but exceeded expectations—a testament to the power of balanced leadership.

The Challenges of Leadership

Leadership within the Void is not without its challenges. Nikolai's confidence and decisiveness, while invaluable, can sometimes overshadow the voices of other personas. His drive for unity can become rigidity, dismissing the messiness and spontaneity that often fuel creativity and innovation.

During another demanding project, Nikolai's insistence on structure left little room for Ravenna's free-flowing ideas. The result was a technically flawless but emotionally hollow presentation. Recognizing this imbalance, I reworked parts of the project, allowing Ravenna's passion to infuse the work with warmth and humanity. The final product struck a chord, proving that leadership requires not just control but adaptability.

Lessons in Leadership

Leading the personas is an evolving practice rooted in intention and self-awareness. Here are the key lessons I've learned in navigating this responsibility:

14. **Create Space for Every Voice**

15. Leadership is not about dominance—it's about ensuring that every persona has the opportunity to contribute. Nikolai's greatest strength lies in listening, balancing each voice to create harmony.

16. *Before tackling a major decision, I pause to reflect on which personas might offer valuable insights. In moments requiring boldness and innovation, Silas and Ravenna often take the lead. For precision and foresight, Isidore steps forward. By giving each persona their moment, I ensure that every perspective is considered.*

17. **Balance Structure with Flexibility**

18. While structure is essential for cohesion, flexibility allows for creativity and growth. Nikolai must temper his drive for control with an openness to the unexpected, allowing the personas to shine in their own ways.

19. *In a brainstorming session, Nikolai's need for order clashed with Ravenna's chaotic but brilliant ideas. By stepping back and giving Ravenna the freedom*

to explore, I uncovered concepts that reshaped the entire project for the better.

20. **Recognize and Address Imbalance**

21. Leadership requires vigilance to ensure that no single persona dominates to the detriment of others. When one voice becomes overpowering, it can lead to burnout, conflict, or missed opportunities.

22. *During a high-pressure week, Silas's relentless energy left little room for Selene's nurturing instincts. Recognizing this, I scheduled time to rest and recharge, allowing Selene to restore balance and prevent exhaustion.*

The Strength of Leadership

The personas' collective power lies in their ability to collaborate, their strengths amplifying each other rather than competing. Nikolai's role as the mediator is essential in harnessing this potential, turning what could be chaos into coherence.

True leadership is not about control—it's about guidance, adaptability, and trust. By honoring each persona's contributions and ensuring balance, Nikolai transforms the Void into a source of creativity, resilience, and achievement.

Lessons for the Future

To my son: If you inherit this gift, know that it is both a privilege and a responsibility. Your personas will offer you extraordinary abilities—creativity that knows no bounds, resilience that carries you through storms, and insight that allows you to see the world in ways others cannot. But these same gifts will test your integrity and resolve, challenging you to lead with wisdom and purpose.

These are the lessons I've learned through my own journey. I offer them to you not as instructions but as a guide to navigating the complexities of multiplicity with courage and grace.

1. Acknowledge the Gift

Your multiplicity is not a burden—it is a unique strength. Embrace it, and you will uncover a wellspring of creativity, resilience, and insight.

Reflection:

There were times when I viewed my personas as obstacles, as voices pulling me in too many directions. It wasn't until I accepted them as integral parts of who I am that I began to understand their value. Each voice within you is a gift waiting to be recognized. Together, they form a mosaic of strength and perspective that is uniquely yours.

2. Understand the Shadows

Each persona carries both light and shadow. **Ravenna's creativity** can become a distraction. **Silas's strength** can turn to aggression. Learn to recognize these dualities, using their strengths while managing their weaknesses.

Reflection:

When Silas's anger threatened to overwhelm me, it was Nikolai's wisdom that reminded me to pause, breathe, and choose my actions carefully. When Ravenna's passion bordered on obsession, it was Noah's stillness that brought me back to balance. Understanding the shadows doesn't mean avoiding them—it means facing them with awareness and care.

3. Lead with Integrity

Act with honesty, empathy, and accountability. Your actions, guided by purpose, will define the legacy of your gift.

Reflection:

Integrity is your anchor, the foundation that ensures your personas work in harmony. When I let Nikolai lead with pride alone, I lost sight of the empathy and compassion needed to connect with others. It was a humbling reminder that leadership is not about control—it's about guiding with purpose and humility.

4. Cultivate Balance

No single persona should dominate. Strive for harmony, allowing each voice to contribute without overshadowing the others.

Reflection:

Balance is not a destination—it is a practice. There were times when Silas's fire burned too brightly or when Isidore's meticulousness stifled creativity. But when all the personas found their place, the result was extraordinary: a symphony of voices, each contributing its part to something greater than the sum of its parts.

5. Learn from Mistakes

You will stumble—this is inevitable. What matters is how you rise, taking responsibility for your actions and learning from every misstep.

Reflection:

I've made mistakes—hurt others with Silas's words, let Elior's ambition cloud my judgment, and allowed Isidore's precision to delay progress. But every misstep taught me something invaluable: the importance of accountability, the strength in apology, and the power of growth. Mistakes are not failures—they are lessons.

A Legacy of Accountability

This gift is not a burden—it is an opportunity. An opportunity to create, to connect, and to leave a lasting impact. It offers the power to shape the world around you, to inspire others, and to turn chaos into something meaningful. But with this opportunity comes a profound responsibility: the responsibility to wield it wisely, with intention and care.

To my son: Let this book serve as both a guide and a reminder. The power within you is immense, but it is not limitless. It will challenge you, and at times, it may feel overwhelming. Yet, when you approach it with purpose and integrity, it will also become your greatest ally.

The Weight of Accountability

The personas within you are not obstacles to be overcome—they are gifts to be understood and harmonized. Each carries its own strengths and shadows, its own lessons to teach. Your responsibility is not to suppress them but to lead them with wisdom, ensuring that their collective power reflects your values.

Reflection:

There were moments in my life when I failed to wield this gift responsibly. Times when Silas's fire burned too brightly or when Isidore's strategy veered into manipulation. Those mistakes taught me that strength without accountability can cause harm, and power without intention can lead to regret. Let these lessons remind you that true power lies not in dominance but in balance and care.

Building a Legacy

The legacy of this gift is not measured by your achievements alone but by the way you use its power to uplift, connect, and create. It is reflected in the relationships you build, the compassion you show, and the wisdom you embody.

> **Create with Purpose**: Use Ravenna's creativity to bring beauty into the world, but temper it with Nikolai's structure to ensure it is meaningful and lasting.

> **Protect with Care**: Let Silas's strength defend what matters most, but guide him with empathy, ensuring that his fire does not consume.

> **Strive with Humility**: Embrace Elior's ambition to push your limits, but balance it with Selene's nurturing instincts, remembering that success is hollow if it comes at the expense of others.

The Force for Good

When guided by purpose and ethics, the chaos within becomes a force for good—a source of light in a world that so often needs it. This gift has the potential to inspire, heal, and create change. But only when wielded with integrity and compassion.

To my son: Build a legacy that reflects not just your strength but your heart. Let your personas challenge you, teach you, and help you grow. Embrace their voices, not as a source of conflict but as a chorus that sings in harmony under your guidance.

This is your opportunity—not just to live with this gift but to thrive with it. To create a life that is extraordinary, purposeful, and true. To leave behind a world touched by your light.

Final Closing Thought

To my son: This is my final message to you, and perhaps the most important one of all. The gift you carry, this multiplicity within you, is not a burden to bear but a treasure to cherish. It is a reflection of the infinite complexity of life itself—beautiful, chaotic, and full of possibility. It is your birthright, your inheritance, and your responsibility.

There will be days when this gift feels like a storm, threatening to pull you under. There will be moments when the voices within you clash, when their demands feel insurmountable, and when the path ahead seems uncertain. In those moments, remember this: you are not defined by the chaos. You are defined by how you choose to navigate it.

You are the center of this symphony, the one who gives the personas purpose and direction. Each of them exists because of you, but you are more than the sum of their parts. You are the anchor, the light, the steady hand that brings order to the storm. And within you lies the power to transform the chaos into something extraordinary.

Do not fear the messiness of this journey. Embrace it. Love every part of yourself—the fierce protector, the quiet observer, the dreamer, the competitor, the leader, the artist, and the nurturer. Each of them has something to teach you, and together, they make you whole.

I won't always be here to guide you, but my words will remain. Let them be your compass when the world feels heavy. Let them remind you that you are not alone and that you carry within you the strength, creativity, and resilience of a thousand lifetimes. Let them give you the courage to face the shadows and the clarity to see the light.

Above all, remember this: balance is not about perfection. It is about compassion—for yourself, for your personas, and for those who walk beside you. It is about learning to dance with the chaos, to find harmony in the discord, and to let that harmony ripple outward into the world.

You are my greatest creation, my legacy, my love. Carry this gift with pride, and use it to create a life that is as beautiful, complex, and meaningful as you are. Wherever this journey takes you, know that I am with you—in every word, in every lesson, and in every moment of your growth.

The world awaits your symphony. Play it boldly.

Chapter 12: A Collection of Wisdom Forged in Harmony

A Collection of Wisdom Forged in Harmony

This collection of wisdom is born from a lifetime spent navigating the complexities of the human mind. These words weren't merely written—they were lived, shaped by the triumphs and struggles of embracing multiplicity, finding balance, and turning inner chaos into strength. Each quote carries a fragment of my journey, a piece of the puzzle that forms the mosaic of who I am.

To my son and to anyone who feels they are more than one, this is my offering to you—a guide to understanding, resilience, and the power that lies in embracing the many faces of yourself. In these reflections, you will find lessons written in the language of survival, love, and hope. May they help you navigate your inner world with courage, compassion, and clarity.

On Embracing Multiplicity

1. *"You are not a singular being—you are a constellation of possibilities."*

2. *"Each face you wear is a reflection of your complexity, not your flaw."*

3. *"Your personas are not masks—they are lenses through which you see the world."*

4. *"Multiplicity is not a burden—it's a gift of adaptability."*

5. *"Your many faces are all facets of the same brilliant gem."*

6. *"To embrace your personas is to embrace the fullness of who you are."*

7. *"You are not fragmented—you are multifaceted."*

8. *"The voices within you are not in conflict; they are in conversation."*

9. *"Each persona carries a piece of your truth—honor them all."*

10. *"You are not less because you are many—you are more."*

On Finding Harmony

1. *"Harmony is not achieved by silencing the voices within but by letting them sing together."*

2. *"Balance is not about control—it's about understanding and integration."*

3. *"True strength lies in uniting your personas, not in denying them."*

4. *"Let your inner orchestra play, but ensure every instrument is in tune."*

5. *"Harmony is the art of giving each persona its rightful place."*

6. *"The symphony of your mind is your greatest masterpiece."*

7.   *"Guiding your personas isn't about dominance—it's about leadership."*

8.   *"Balance is the bridge between chaos and creation."*

9.   *"When your personas work together, they create a force greater than the sum of their parts."*

10. *"Harmony is the light that transforms inner conflict into inner strength."*

On Self-Discovery

1.   *"The journey to know yourself begins with listening to every part of you."*

2.   *"Self-discovery is not about erasing your complexities—it's about embracing them."*

3.   *"To understand yourself is to understand the many lives you carry within."*

4.   *"Your true self isn't hidden—it's found in the spaces between your personas."*

5.   *"Exploring your inner world is the greatest adventure you'll ever take."*

6.   *"Every persona tells a story—listen, and you'll uncover your narrative."*

7.   *"The path to self-discovery is paved with curiosity and courage."*

8.   *"You are not defined by a single face but by the depth of all your faces."*

9. *"Your identity is not fixed—it is a journey of constant evolution."*

10. *"Self-discovery is the art of weaving your fragments into a beautiful whole."*

On Strength and Resilience

1. *"Strength is not found in avoiding struggle but in rising through it."*

2. *"Your personas are not your weaknesses—they are your allies in resilience."*

3. *"Every challenge is an opportunity to call forth the strength within."*

4. *"The resilience you seek is already inside you, waiting to be awakened."*

5. *"When you fall, let your personas help you rise."*

6. *"The shadows within you are not dark—they are powerful forces of growth."*

7. *"True resilience is found in accepting all parts of yourself, even the difficult ones."*

8. *"Your strength lies in your ability to adapt and evolve."*

9. *"When the world tests you, remember: you carry many strengths within."*

10. *"You are unbreakable because you are not one thing—you are many."*

On Navigating Challenges

1. *"Challenges don't define you—they refine you."*

2. *"When one persona struggles, let another offer its strength."*

3. *"The greatest challenges reveal the greatest truths about who you are."*

4. *"When you face chaos, remember: you are the conductor, not the orchestra."*

5. *"Every problem is an opportunity for your personas to collaborate."*

6. *"Your inner world may be complex, but it holds the solutions you need."*

7. *"The storm within is not your enemy—it's your teacher."*

8. *"Challenges are not walls—they are doors waiting to be opened."*

9. *"Let your personas guide you through the maze of life, each one lighting the way."*

10. *"Every obstacle is a lesson in disguise, placed there to help you grow."*

On Identity and Self-Worth

1. *"You are not defined by your personas—they are defined by you."*

2. *"Your worth is not diminished by your complexity; it is enhanced by it."*

3.   *"You are not fragmented—you are a masterpiece in progress."*

4.   *"Your identity is not a puzzle to solve—it is a story to be lived."*

5.   *"You are the sum of all your parts, and together, they make you whole."*

6.   *"The many faces of you are not contradictions—they are expressions of your depth."*

7.   *"Your self-worth is not tied to any single part of you—it is found in your entirety."*

8.   *"Who you are is not fixed—it is as limitless as your imagination."*

9.   *"You are not too much—you are exactly enough."*

10.   *"Your identity is a garden—nurture every part of it."*

On Legacy and Impact

1.   *"Your legacy is not in what you achieve but in the understanding you pass on."*

2.   *"The way you navigate your inner world will guide others through theirs."*

3.   *"Your personas are your gift to the world—use them to create, connect, and inspire."*

4.   *"The impact you make is not measured by your perfection but by your authenticity."*

5.   *"What you leave behind is the understanding you bring to those around you."*

6. *"Your legacy is found in the harmony you create within yourself and share with others."*

7. *"Let your journey inspire those who walk beside you."*

8. *"The wisdom you gain from your personas is a light for others to follow."*

9. *"Your story is your legacy—write it with courage and love."*

10. *"You are not alone, and your legacy will remind others of that truth."*

On Living Fully

1. *"Life is not meant to be simple—it is meant to be full."*

2. *"Live every moment with the fullness of who you are."*

3. *"Your personas are not holding you back—they are propelling you forward."*

4. *"Each day is a new opportunity to explore the depths of your mind."*

5. *"The many faces of you are your passport to a richer, more dynamic life."*

6. *"To live fully is to embrace every voice within you."*

7. *"You are not confined by your inner world—you are expanded by it."*

8. *"Let your personas be your guides to a life of meaning and purpose."*

9. *"Live boldly, knowing you carry a symphony of strengths within you."*

10. *"Your life is not a single note—it is a symphony waiting to be played."*

On Love and Connection

1. *"Love yourself first, for only then can you truly love others."*

2. *"Your complexity is a gift to those who truly see you."*

3. *"Connection begins with understanding, both within and without."*

4. *"The people who matter will love every part of you, shadows and all."*

5. *"Your personas are not barriers to love—they are bridges."*

6. *"Share your journey, and you will find those who walk beside you."*

7. *"Let your story inspire connection, not isolation."*

8. *"Love is not about perfection—it is about presence."*

9. *"You are not too complex to be loved—you are made to be understood."*

10. *"Connection is found in honesty and the courage to be seen."*

Final Wisdom

1. *"Your journey is your own, but it is not yours alone."*

2. *"Every persona is a part of the legacy you leave behind."*

3. *"The many faces of you are not separate—they are the facets of your greatness."*

4. *"You are a tapestry of stories woven together into something extraordinary."*

5. *"The greatest gift you can give the world is the harmony you create within yourself."*

6. *"Do not fear the shadows—they are where your light shines brightest."*

7. *"Your mind is not a battlefield—it is a masterpiece in progress."*

8. *"The personas are not your masters—they are your tools for living fully."*

9. *"You are not just one face—you are infinite possibilities, and that is your power."*

Epilogue

My Dearest son,

As I write these final words, I am overcome with emotion—pride, love, fear, and hope intertwine in a way that words alone cannot fully express. This journey, both mine and now yours, has been one of unimaginable complexity. It is a journey of shadows and light, of chaos and harmony, and it is a journey I would not trade for anything.

You are my greatest creation, my truest legacy. As I reflect on the struggles I have endured—the battles fought within and the scars left behind—I realize they were never just for me. They were for you. Every step I took through the darkness, every moment I stood at the edge of despair and chose to keep going, was so I could hand you the tools to navigate your own path.

The Shadows That Shaped Me

The shadows within me have not been kind. They have been relentless, demanding, and, at times, terrifying. There were days when I didn't know who I was when the personas pulled me in so many directions that I felt like a stranger in my own skin. Wrath would rage, tearing apart what I'd tried so hard to build. Lust would whisper temptations that distracted me from my goals. Pride would blind me, leading me to stumble, while Greed's hunger for control consumed me.

But through it all, I learned. Slowly painfully, I found the strength to understand the shadows instead of fighting them. I realized that these personas weren't my enemies—they were my teachers. Each one reflected a part of me I needed to confront, embrace, and balance.

Silas taught me that strength isn't about destroying what stands in your way—it's about protecting what matters most. Ravenna showed me that vulnerability and creativity are not weaknesses but the essence of connection. Isidore reminded me that foresight and strategy are powerful tools, but only when wielded with compassion. And Nikolai—the anchor of it all—taught me that leadership isn't about control; it's about harmony, about guiding rather than dominating.

But these lessons didn't come easily. They came through sleepless nights, through tears shed in solitude, through relationships I broke and had to rebuild. They came through moments when I questioned my worth, my sanity, and my ability to be the father you deserve.

A Father's Love

If there is one thing I need you to understand, it is this: every struggle I faced, every battle I fought, was driven by one unshakable truth—I love you more than words can say. Even before you were born, I carried the weight of this gift, knowing it could one day be yours. I didn't just want to survive it—I wanted to master it so I could guide you, so I could show you that even the darkest shadows can lead to light.

There were times when I doubted myself. How could I teach you to navigate this gift when I was still learning? How could I protect you from the pain I knew too well? But love has a way of quieting doubt, of reminding us that we are stronger than we believe. So I kept going—for you, for the legacy I wanted to leave, for the hope that you would never feel as lost as I once did.

Your Journey Awaits

My son, I do not know what lies ahead for you. I cannot predict whether you will inherit this gift, nor can I foresee the challenges you will face. But I do know this: you are stronger than you think, braver than you feel, and more capable than you realize.

If you ever find yourself standing where I once stood, looking into the shadows and wondering if you will ever find your way, remember this: the shadows are not there to consume you. They are there to shape you, to teach you, and to make you whole.

You will face moments of doubt, moments when the personas feel like burdens rather than gifts. In those moments, pause. Breathe. Listen. The answers are within you, waiting to be uncovered. Trust in yourself, and trust in the strength of the personas that walk with you.

A Legacy of Balance and Love

The greatest lesson I can leave you is the importance of balance. Let Silas protect you, but never let him hurt those you love. Let Ravenna inspire you, but don't let her passions consume you. Let Isidore plan your path, but remember to leave room for spontaneity and joy. Let Nikolai guide you, but don't be afraid to question him when necessary.

You are not just one voice—you are many. And when those voices harmonize, they create something extraordinary.

This is your legacy, my son—not just the personas but the strength, love, and courage they bring. Carry it with pride but also with humility. Use it not just to build your own life but to uplift those around you. Be the light in someone else's darkness, the calm in their storm, the hope in their despair.

A Father's Hope

To my son: As you step into the world, remember that you are never alone. You carry within you the lessons of those who came before you, the strength of the personas that walk with you, and the love of a father who believes in you with every fiber of his being.

This book is not just a guide—it is a testament to what is possible. It is proof that even in the face of chaos, we can find harmony. Even in the deepest shadows, we can find light. And even when we feel broken, we are capable of creating something whole and beautiful.

I am proud of you, my son. More than words can ever express. Carry this gift with honor, and know that no matter where your journey takes you, I am with you—in every shadow, in every moment of light, in every step you take.

The world is waiting for you. Go and leave it better than you found it.

With all my heart,

Your Father

The End